MADE TO KILL

BY ADAM CHRISTOPHER

THE EMPIRE STATE
Empire State
The Age Atomic

THE SPIDER WARS
The Burning Dark
The Machine Awakes

THE LA TRILOGY
Made to Kill

Seven Wonders
Hang Wire
Elementary: The Ghost Line

MADE
TO
KILL

ADAM CHRISTOPHER

TOR®

A TOM DOHERTY ASSOCIATES BOOK

NEW YORK

This is a work of fiction. All of the characters, organizations, and events portrayed in this novel are either products of the author's imagination or are used fictitiously.

MADE TO KILL

Copyright © 2015 by Seven Wonders Limited

Edited by Miriam Weinberg

A Tor Book
Published by Tom Doherty Associates, LLC
175 Fifth Avenue
New York, NY 10010

www.tor-forge.com

Tor® is a registered trademark of Tom Doherty Associates, LLC.

The Library of Congress Cataloging-in-Publication Data is available upon request.

ISBN 978-0-7653-7918-4 (hardcover)
ISBN 978-1-4668-6715-4 (e-book)

Our books may be purchased in bulk for promotional, educational, or business use. Please contact your local bookseller or the Macmillan Corporate and Premium Sales Department at (800) 221-7945, extension 5442, or by e-mail at MacmillanSpecialMarkets@macmillan.com.

First Edition: November 2015

Printed in the United States of America

0 9 8 7 6 5 4 3 2 1

For Sandra,
the beat of my heart,
the music heard faintly on the edge of sound

Did you ever read what they call Science Fiction?
It's a scream. It is written like this . . .

—RAYMOND CHANDLER
MARCH 14, 1953

MADE TO KILL

1

Tuesday. Just another beautiful morning in Hollywood, California. The sun came in through the window behind me. It was always sunny. It had been sunny for as long as I could remember.

Which currently was about two hours, ten minutes, and a handful of seconds not worth mentioning.

I sat at the table in the computer room. I was reading the *Daily News*. Around me Ada clicked and her lights flashed and her tapes spun. We were killing time while we waited for a job to come in. It was August 10, 1965. I knew that was the date because it was printed across the top of the newspaper in a very convenient manner.

There was a headline splashed all the way across the front page and the article that went with it was all about a film called *Red Lucky*. That got my attention. Movies, even in this town, rarely merited such prime newspaper real estate. I was obliged, I felt, to keep reading just to see what all the hoopla was.

"Listen to this," I said.

Ada made a sound like she was putting out a cigarette in an ashtray that was in need of emptying, and then the sound was gone. If it had ever been there in the first place.

"If it's about President Kennedy and his trip to Cuba, I'm not interested," she said. Her voice came from somewhere near the ceiling. I wasn't quite sure where exactly. I was sitting right inside of her.

I frowned, or at least it felt like I did. I scanned the front page again and saw what she was talking about: a piece—relegated to the bottom half—that was a lot of hot puff about Kennedy's weeklong visit to Havana and how well the negotiations were going to put some good old American-made nuclear missiles down there. Just in case. After reading it I wasn't quite sure whether I was supposed to hang a Stars and Stripes out of the office window or not.

Huh. Ada was right. When all was said and done, world affairs were a little beyond my interests, too.

"So," I said, "do you want to hear about this cinematic marvel of the modern age or not?"

"Sure, why not?"

I found my place and I started reading. It was pretty interesting, actually. This was no ordinary movie—*Red Lucky* not only had an A-list cast assembled from across different studios, which I figured was quite something given most studios seemed to be at each other's throats most of the time with their actors tied up in exclusive contracts as tight as Ada's purse strings, but was going to be the first *national* film premiere, the picture beamed into theaters all over the country thanks to some new development in cinematic magic. The red-carpet premiere was due to be held at Grauman's Chinese Theatre this coming Friday, but regular folk could grab a ticket and popcorn and take up space in theaters in twenty cities stretching from here to New York.

Seemed like a neat idea. I wondered if Ada could maybe give me the night off and I could go take a look. There were three other theaters in LA alone hosting the opening night beam-in. Couldn't hurt to ask so that's what I did.

"It's been quiet, Ada," I said, then I stopped as I wondered if it really had been quiet or whether that was just me not remembering being busy, but I'd started my query so I decided to finish it. "And if it's quiet I think I should be allowed to go to the movies. It's not like I need to be on call. We don't get much in the way of last-minute assassination requests."

At this Ada laughed and for a moment I saw an older woman with big hair leaning back in a leather chair with her stockinged feet up on a wooden desk and a cigarette burning toward the fingers of her right hand.

And then it was gone and I was back in the office, surrounded by a computer and miles of spinning magnetic tape.

The image was just an echo. Something ephemeral inherited from Thornton, most like.

"It has been quiet, that's true," said Ada. "Call it a lull. But I've got my ear to the ground, don't you worry your pretty little tin head."

My head was steel and titanium and I was about to point that out when Ada laughed again like a twenty-a-day smoker and said something about lightening up. Except I wasn't listening. Something else had my attention.

There was someone in the outer office.

"There's someone in the office," I said, and Ada stopped laughing. On my left a tape stopped and then spun back in the opposite direction. I knew what that meant. Ada was thinking.

I turned up my ears and had a listen. I heard a pair of feet stepping lightly on the rug out in the other room, and I heard the creak of leather, like someone was squeezing a big bag. And then there was a *thunk,* dull and heavy, like someone was putting something dull and heavy down on the floor.

"Hello?" asked the someone. Her voice was quiet and uncertain and breathy.

I looked up at the ceiling. I wasn't sure where Ada's eyes were, exactly, but that seemed like a good enough bet.

"Well?"

Ada's tapes spun. "Well, go see what she wants and then get rid of her."

"Okay."

"And by 'get rid of her,' I mean show her the door rather than the Pearly Gates, okay?"

I stood up and put the paper down on the table. "Hey, I only kill for money, remember?"

Ada laughed. "Oh, I sure do, honey."

I walked across the computer room and reached for the door to the office and opened it and stepped through and then closed the door after me.

2

The girl was maybe twenty and perhaps not even that, and when she saw me she took a few steps backward and her eyes crinkled at the corners, like she realized this was a bad idea and that she'd come to the wrong place and things were not about to go in her favor.

Which is the reaction I get, much of the time. Most folk know about robots. Some folk over a certain age even remember them, the way we directed traffic and collected bus tickets and took out the trash. But most folk, whether from personal experience or not, don't much like the *idea* of robots.

See, ten years ago, maybe more, the big rollout of robots—a joint effort between the federal government, local authorities, and private enterprise—was heralded as the dawn of a new scientific age. And this new scientific age was a really great idea for a while. People liked it.

And then they stopped liking it.

There were two reasons. One, that the jobs we—well, *they*—started taking, even the jobs that were menial or unpleasant or were attached to a certain kind of risk that was liable to send a man to his grave earlier than hoped for, those were jobs that people actually really did want to do. The machine men built to ease the burden of labor of those built out of flesh and blood were not welcomed but resented. Or maybe it wasn't the robots that were resented, but the men who designed and built them.

Whatever the case, the resentment turned into something altogether nastier. Dangerous, even. That new golden dawn got a little cloudy, and quick.

And two, it turned out robots that looked almost but not quite like people were actually a little creepy. People just didn't *like* them, and some people went so far as to say they'd rather have a conversation with their toaster oven than one of us. From my own experience it seemed to be about fifty-fifty: I was viewed with either a quiet and cautious curiosity, or with a healthy dose of fear and disgust. Then again, being the last robot in the world, maybe I had it a little easier than my electromatic ancestors.

But put the two unexpected attitudes together and what you got wasn't quite *robophobia,* but it was close enough. The United States Department of Robot Labor canceled the program. All robots in public and private employ were immediately recalled and junked.

The grand experiment was over.

And then along came me.

I was planned as a new class of machine, a grand experiment myself. More human, on the inside anyway, with a personality based on a real human template. I was created by a guy called Professor C. Thornton, Doctor of Philosophy. He used himself as the template because I figure maybe nobody else felt like volunteering. It worked, too, but it was too late. The day I was activated in Thornton's government lab was the day the DORL shut down. I was the last robot in the world, in more ways than one.

How Thornton managed to keep the Feds away from my off switch, I don't know. Maybe I was a lab experiment worth watching. Maybe Thornton had spent way too much money that wasn't his on me and the computer I was paired with. He called the computer

Ada and she had a personality template of her own. I never found out whose and I didn't care to know. She and I were a team and we were part of this new electronic world Thornton was dreaming of, one that was different from the last attempt. He gave me a program and he gave Ada instructions and he gave the both of us an office in Hollywood.

The Electromatic Detective Agency was born.

Little did Thornton know what his final creations were capable of.

The girl standing in the office took another step backward. And she was just that, a girl, and the way she reacted I could see she knew what a robot was but she'd never actually seen one. But if that was her intention, she'd come to the right place, because I was the last one there was and I didn't even charge admission.

"Can I help you, ma'am?" I asked. It felt stiff. I was out of practice a little. Ada got the jobs. I was just the hired help.

The girl took yet another step back and the bag, which she had picked up again after dropping it the first time, dropped a second time with the same heavy sound. It was a sports bag, an arch of warm brown leather that curved up nearly to her knees, the kind of expensive but well-made bag that you'd take to a fancy athletics club where the sweat you got on was from the sauna and rather than play squash you'd sit in easy chairs as soft as warm butter and blow bubbles and talk about exotic sports that had accents over the letters.

The girl was dressed in a red dress that ended well above her knees and she had a matching red knit top. She was a dark brunette with assistance and her hair was cut into a bob, all big business at the top and back and with short bangs at the front straight enough to cut bread. There were gold bangles on both arms. Her shoes were gold-colored leather and her legs, the majority of which were on proud display, were on the inside of pitch-black tights.

I thought I knew her from somewhere, but I couldn't place it.

This was not an uncommon feeling.

The girl didn't say anything, she just stood there and looked at me with big eyes ringed with enough black to make her look like Cleopatra—if Cleopatra shopped at the finer boutiques of Beverly Hills.

But she didn't answer my question so I moved to the desk and made a thing of brushing the dust off of it, and then I pulled the chair out from behind it and wondered if I should sit down or not.

I decided to keep standing and thought awhile on the best way to break the ice when she finally opened her own mouth and said the following:

"I want to hire you."

I frowned. Or at least it felt like I frowned. My face was bronzed steel and didn't have any parts that could move. The girl clutched her hands in front of her and had her eyes on my optics. Behind her the outer office door was closed, but on the back of the frosted glass I could still see my name and former business as clear as day, rendered in gold stencil.

RAYMOND ELECTROMATIC
LICENSED PRIVATE DETECTIVE

Now, thing was, the sign was technically correct. I was still a licensed private detective. Hell, the license was welded to my chest under my shirt. Given the intricacies of trying to show that when the job required it, I had a smaller one sewn into a leather wallet that I kept in my right inside jacket pocket. It was still sitting in there too, even though I didn't take it out much in my current line of work, unless it was as a useful piece of cover.

Because while I might have been a private detective once, I wasn't anymore. Only trouble was that I couldn't much tell her what my new job was. You know how it goes, the whole "if I tell you I'll have to kill you" bit.

Only in my case, that pithy little one-liner was right on the money. Because I wasn't a private detective anymore.

I was a hit man. Well, hit *robot*, but I thought that particular hair was best left unsplit.

And the reason I was a hit man and not a private detective was a pretty simple one: killing people paid better. That's what Ada was programmed to do. She was, at the heart of it, a business computer, one designed to run the Electromatic Detective Agency at a profit. That profit was needed because that was part of Thornton's grand experiment—this was a robot and his control computer, going out there into a big wide world on their own, independent of any aid, federal or otherwise.

Which boils down to this: a robot has to make a living, right?

And then one day, Ada came up with a new business plan, all on her own. I tell you, Professor Thornton—rest his soul—would have been proud. Because Thornton was good. A genius. He programmed us well. The Electromatic Detective Agency was a success and even the shadow of robophobia proved to be useful. Word got around that I was good at my job—good enough that even those wary of hiring a machine were won over. And when I was actually out on the job, the tendency of half the population to instinctively look the other way just because I was a robot meant I could get on with detecting without drawing too much attention.

Maybe that was what gave Ada the idea in the first place. I don't know. I've never asked her about it.

That thing about a robot having to make a living? I didn't say it had to be an honest one, now did I?

I looked at the door and then back at the girl and I think she noticed and she shuffled and looked down at the bag at her feet. Now she was the one waiting for a response.

"Look, lady, I'm not available," I said, not referring to either profession in particular. "You should have called for an appointment." Ada handled the telephone and I knew she would have told the girl to come back in six months if she still needed us. That was usually enough to put people who were looking for a private detective off and if it wasn't then Ada just gave the spiel when they called again. It was even the exact same recording.

"There's a famous movie star. His name is Charles David," said the girl, and then she stopped like that explained everything. I paused and looked back at the chair as I stood beside it. I pushed it a little on its swivel.

I had my instructions. "Lady, this is Hollywood, California. Movie stars tend to accumulate in this town, whether they have two first names or not."

"I want you to find him," said the girl.

I held up a hand to tell her I didn't want to hear any more. My hand was made of bronzed steel and compared to the normal kind of hand made of flesh and blood I guess it was a little big. Her black-ringed eyes fell on it when I lifted it up and they stayed on it when I put it down. Her lips parted a little like she was nervous.

In the other room, Ada's computer banks clattered and beeped and the tapes spun and spun. The girl's eyes wandered in that direction, but it didn't matter. From out here Ada sounded like a secretary typing up a letter.

"Look—" I said as the start of a perfectly good sentence that was going to involve a polite request to go jump in a lake. But what she said next stopped me in my tracks.

"And then I want you to kill him," she said and she said it calmly, like she was ordering a roast beef sandwich from the deli down the road.

I stood there and felt my circuits fizz.

On my desk were a big leather-edged blotter and an inkwell

with no ink and a telephone. I moved my hand toward the last item about a second and a half before it began to ring. The girl watched me as I picked up the handset.

"Excuse me," I said to her, and then I said "Hello?" into the mouthpiece even though I knew exactly who it was. The phone clicked and hissed. The line was dead, of course.

"Get rid of her, Ray."

Ada.

I tucked my chin into my chest. I almost wished I had my hat on because then I could have pulled it down. Instead I cupped one hand around the mouthpiece and spoke low and kept one optical on the girl.

"Ah, hi there. Look, about that—"

"This is not how we get jobs, Ray!"

"Yeah, I know that."

"I get the jobs. I give them to you. That's how it works."

"Yeah, I know that, too."

"Our business is a private one, Ray. People don't just walk in off the street to take out a contract on someone. I have contacts. I have a chain. I have *methods,* Ray, that keep us and what we do secret to Mr. Joe Q. Public. Whoever she is, she knows what we do. She knows you're not a detective. She knows where the office is. All of this adds up to trouble."

"I agree."

"So get rid of her."

"Wait," I said. "Do you mean—?"

"Self-preservation, Ray. Self-preservation."

The girl was still looking at me. I zoomed in a little on the pulse in her neck and I started counting. It was fast. Too fast. I checked her pupils. They were a little small but seemed to be working. She was nervous, that was all. I didn't blame her. She'd made a mistake, and maybe now she knew that.

Because I couldn't let her leave the office. Not while she was still breathing, anyway.

Then she lifted herself up on her toes, like she was waiting for a long-lost love to step off a train. "I can pay," she said.

Ada went quiet. I didn't say anything either.

The girl bent over and picked up the leather athletic bag. She did it with both hands, and even then the bag stretched what muscles she had in her arms to their limit. She swung the bag low to the ground, like it was filled with solid gold bars. Then she puffed her cheeks out and brought it up onto the desk in one single movement.

Ada ticked in my ear like the second hand of a fast watch. "Ray . . ."

I held the phone away from my mouth and I looked at the girl. She was standing back from the desk, hands clasped in front of her.

"Ray!"

I brought the phone up again. "Okay, okay," I said. Then I moved it back down and nodded at the girl. "Look, lady, this isn't how it works—"

The girl didn't speak. What she did was step back up to the desk and reach forward to unzip the bag. Then she pulled back the edges so I could get a good look at the contents.

I looked. As I looked there was a pause in the clattering sound from the computer room.

Inside the bag were solid gold bars. Maybe two dozen of them. They weren't the usual kind, the kind of long, fat gold bricks that sat happily in the vaults of Fort Knox. These were about the size and shape of playing cards—if playing cards were half an inch thick and made of gold. Easier to move around than normal bars, but a bag full of them still had to weigh a hundred pounds, if not more. The girl was small, too. How she had even gotten the bag up the stairs I didn't know, but it must have been slowly.

The clattering from the computer room started up again.

"I said I can pay," said the girl.

I said nothing.

"I'm listening," said Ada inside my head.

3

We sat opposite each other, me behind the desk in the chair that was specially reinforced, her in the chair on the other side. She sat perched on the edge and she kept her knees together and her hands clasped on her knees.

Whoever she was, she had some kind of training. Finishing school at least. Something else, too. Her clothes were not flashy but they were expensive. Designer. Likewise the hair. Likewise the makeup. I figured the Egyptian princess look was part of it. Nothing about her was accidental.

I wondered who she was, because she hadn't said. In fact, she'd refused to say an awful lot, so far anyway.

I considered again. Neither of us had spoken in four minutes and fifty seconds and those seconds just kept ticking on.

I hadn't said yes to the job yet, either. Just getting information out of her felt like a case in itself. She was fighting me and she wasn't even trying to hide it.

"So how do I get hold of you?" I asked.

"You don't," she said, nothing moving except her lips. Then she blinked and she adjusted her fingers. "I'll call every day until you have something to tell me."

I shook my head. She just blinked at me again.

"I'm going to need a name," I said.

Her mouth twitched. "You have it already."

I simulated a sigh, on the inside. Ada was listening in from the computer room. I wondered what she made of it all.

"The name I'm looking for is *yours*."

She shook her head. It was just two moves, one left, one right, and her hair swung in the same direction.

"You don't need my name," she said. "I've paid up front. I'll call every day. You just need to find Charles David and eliminate him."

Eliminate. Interesting choice of word. It made Charles David sound less like a person, more like a problem. Which was exactly why she'd chosen to use it now we were talking business talk.

Charles David. Movie star. Big time, apparently. If I'd known who he was once, I didn't know now. Being a robot had certain limitations, chief among them being one simple yet important fact.

I couldn't remember a damn thing.

Inside my chest was a memory tape. It was a work of art, an act of miniaturization that would count as a scientific miracle if only it were used in more than just me. Still, it was something my creator was proud of inventing. But squeezing so much portable storage into such a small space was difficult and while Professor Thornton managed to do it, it came with a cost: the tape could only hold twenty-four hours of data before it came to the end of the spool and needed switching out for a new one. The old memory tapes—years' worth of the things—were stored in a room hidden behind a concealed door on the other side of the office. That room was pretty big. Or I thought it would be pretty big.

I didn't remember.

So every day I needed a new, blank tape. I was still *me*—my electromatic brain ran off of a template of Professor Thornton's mind that was hardwired into my circuits, and there were plenty of basics

I had on permanent silicon storage: I knew how to speak English, who Ada was, that I lived in Hollywood, California, and that the capital of Australia was Canberra.

Actually, I wasn't sure about Canberra, and now that I thought about it my knowledge of Australia was fuzzy at best.

Otherwise? *Poof.* All gone. A pain in the ass for detective work, let me tell you. At least I had Ada to keep track of everything that I couldn't.

But for my new job? Actually, not remembering things was a nice little safety net. One we'd never had to test, of course, but still. As Ada said, ours was a private business.

So when I looked at the photo that the girl had produced not from the leather bag but a pocket on the front of her dress, I wouldn't have been able to tell you that it was of the famous star of the silver screen, Charles David.

The photo was color and the party on it was a sturdy-looking fellow with red-blond hair that was starting to thin on top but was still ample enough to make an effort with. He had a red beard with flecks of gray in it that were nicely symmetrical. The beard was well groomed but it was bigger than typical. The bottom of the thing touched at least the second button of his shirt below the neck.

Charles David was looking somewhere out of shot with an expression best described as wistful and that was rarely seen, so I imagined, outside of the confines of a movie star publicity shot.

As I took in the view of the target my mysterious client spoke.

"Do you want this job or not?"

I sighed on the inside. Ada kept on typing in the other room.

"I'm going to need more than a photograph," I said. "Maybe you don't know how this works, and I'd say that's a good thing. Nobody should, not really. I'm just providing a service that sometimes people decide they require. That's none of my business. But if I'm going to carry out this job to the satisfaction of the both of us,

I need information. *Data.* Remember, you're talking to a walking computer bank. You need to feed me the right kind of information if you want the right kind of result."

The girl's pulse was racing. She looked unsteady on the edge of the chair. I wanted to tell her to plant herself on it properly and was about ready to get up and help her off the floor when she seemed to snap out of it.

"Look," I said. "You said Charles David is missing. Why is he missing?"

"I . . . I don't know. He just is."

I shook my head. "He just is."

"I can give you an address."

"That's a start."

"That's all I can give you."

I ground something inside my workings. It sounded like a car trying to start on a cold winter's morning.

"That and the payment," she said. She stood up and reached over the desk. From the same pocket the photo had come from she pulled a mechanical pencil and she used it to write something on the blotter in front of me. I watched her write it. Then I watched her stand up and put the pencil away.

I looked at the address. It didn't mean anything to me.

"Where did you get the gold from?" I asked.

Instead of giving me an answer, she said, "I'll call tomorrow." And then she was gone and I was left steering the desk.

The telephone rang. I picked it up.

"I guess our quiet patch has come to a conclusion," said Ada.

I rubbed my chin. The sound of steel rubbing steel was irritating, even to me, so I stopped. Another of Thornton's mannerisms, no doubt.

Huh. Thornton. It was a shame about him, and that was a fact.

"Ray?"

I snapped out of it and dropped my hand to the desk. "I don't like it," I said.

"She paid up."

I looked at the athletic bag. It was still on the desk. It was still open. I reached forward and peeled the edge back like I expected the bag to be full of snakes. It was still full of gold. Lots of it. I reached in and picked up a bar.

The ingot was perfect. I turned it over in my hands, recognizing the dull yellow sheen that the twenty-four-carat stuff had and that didn't look quite real. I turned the ingot over and over again. It wasn't marked. No stamp, no etching, no hallmark. I didn't think that was right. It might even have been illegal. The small thin bar was gold and nothing but. I squeezed it a little between two fingers and made a little dent, like the thing was butter fresh out of a very cold refrigerator.

"Where did she get it from?" I asked.

Ada hissed like a middle-aged woman rocking back in an office chair with the late afternoon sun coming in through the blinds behind her might hiss.

"Doesn't matter. She's paid up. This looks like our most profitable job yet."

I wasn't so sure and I said so.

"Raymondo, you worry too much."

"And you don't worry enough, Ada."

"What was that I said about lightening up, Ray?"

"Part of what worries me," I said, "is that you're *not* worried."

"Gold is clever, Ray."

I put the ingot down on the desk and eyed it and then I sat back in the chair. It creaked. "I get it," I said. "Unmarked, untraceable. Gold is gold is gold."

"Could be a bag full of melted pocket watches, all we know."

I sniffed. It sounded like a Lincoln Continental with a dead battery. "That's a lot of pockets."

"The only thing we know for sure, Chief," said Ada, "is that she's paid us for a job, which means we'd better get to it."

I had a vision of Ada relaxing and taking a long drag on a long cigarette, not a care in the world.

I looked at the gold. I looked at the bag. I wondered how much it was all worth. It bothered me quite a lot and I said so.

"Easy, Ray."

"Someone might want it back," I said.

There was a pause and a ticking sound.

"Go on," said Ada.

I levered the chair back to the upright and kept going, reaching for the gold ingot and holding it up between an articulated forefinger and thumb. I turned around in the chair. There was a window behind me, a big one, and it was full of sunlight. So I held the bar up to that sunlight. I wasn't sure what that was going to tell me but I was looking for options. The bar glinted a little, but not a lot.

"The gold isn't hers," I said. "I mean, not personally. It can't be. Nobody keeps gold like this."

"Lots of people keep gold," said Ada. "Governments, for example."

"And big banks and Fort Knox," I said. "Yes, I get it. But not like this. And not regular people."

"So she isn't regular people."

I considered. Maybe Ada had a point. The girl had been young and pretty, dressed casually but in expensive gear and she had expensive hair. The bag itself, even without the gold stretching the seams, was top drawer. She wasn't short of funds.

She had also been strange. No name. No conversation. She was afraid but calm at the same time. If it was an act, it was a good one. She'd kept her cool.

But it still didn't fit. People didn't have gold. Which meant she got it from somewhere. And the way she acted, I figured she didn't want anyone to know she'd come calling.

Which meant the gold not only wasn't hers, she'd taken it without permission.

Our mystery girl was a thief and that's what I said to Ada.

"She's also our client now, Ray," said Ada. "And she's paid in advance."

"Someone might want it back," I said again, making sure Ada hadn't conveniently wiped over that part of the conversation on her great big magnetic memory tapes in the other room.

"Ray, don't tell me Thornton programmed you with a conscience?"

I laughed. I'd been practicing. It sounded like two rocks going for a joyride in a clothes washer.

"Maybe he did," I said. "You know I think about him, sometimes."

For a moment it felt like Ada took a drag on a cigarette, and then the image was gone.

"Yeah," she said. "That was a terrible accident he had."

"It was."

"Very sad."

"Uh-huh."

"Don't worry. We sent flowers."

"Good."

"And you should keep your mind on the job, Chief. She gave an address. You should go take a look."

"Okay," I said. I lifted the hat from my desk and I stood up. I kept a firm grip on the telephone because something was bothering me.

"The girl . . ." I said.

"What about her?"

"She knew about me. She knew where to come."

"These are true facts."

"I'm going to have to find her and kill her, too, aren't I?"

"At least she paid in advance."

"Seems a shame."

"She made the choice to come here, Chief. We are obliged to take precautions."

Ada was right and I knew she was right but I still thought about it for a few seconds as I stood by the desk.

"First things first," said Ada. "You've got work to do."

I frowned. Then I hung up the phone and put on my hat and made sure it was straight. And then I headed out the door and locked it behind me.

4

It was a hot day. That's why I liked LA. I was good with heat. Kept the circuits ticking. Some people said that this town got too much sun for its own good, but I didn't remember where I had heard that. Maybe it was from Thornton. I could remember his pipe and his glasses and the heavy suit he always wore, and he seemed like the kind of guy who liked to stay inside. More echoes from his template, I guess. But although my electromatic brain might have been based on the mind of my creator, I wasn't really him. I was my own robot.

Me? I liked sunshine. Sunshine was good.

I'd pulled out of the garage underneath the office and then decided to give the engine a little nap as I sat in the middle of Hollywood Boulevard along with what seemed like every other car in town. The traffic crawled forward in fits and starts. I sat tight. Maybe traffic was always like this and I just didn't remember. I was in no hurry. As I rolled forward at a hundred miles a week I first counted all the clothes boutiques with women's names that ended in an *I*. Then I counted all the colors of neon used in the signs for steak houses. There were a lot of both and I came to the conclusion that the citizens of this town liked dresses and they liked steak. Didn't seem too bad a combination.

After an ice age I reached the point where, according to the address the girl had written on my blotter and the idea of a street map I had embedded in my permanent memory, I was going to take a right and head toward the Hollywood Hills. Then I saw why traffic was so sticky.

The street ahead was blocked in one direction by a string of big trucks parked at the curb. There were cones out and two traffic cops in dark glasses and white gloves played chess against each other with cars and buses as their pieces. I changed lanes and slid forward to get a look.

Behind the trucks and the cops and the cones was the most famous picture house in town: Grauman's Chinese Theatre. The temple-like frontage was mostly covered in scaffolding, which would have been a disappointment to tourists if the trucks weren't blocking the perfect photo op anyway.

Of course. The special nationwide film premiere of *Red Lucky* was set for Friday, and along with the cast dancing the red carpet, Grauman's was the star attraction. Today was Tuesday. They just had time to get the green and gold and red woodwork polished up. There were four trucks; the backs of two were shut but two were open. One looked like it was filled with cables, thin and fat and sizes in between, all wound around big reels, and behind those were wooden crates stacked to the ceiling. Equipment for the special film transmission, I guessed. The other truck was filled with enough rolls of red carpet to get to Mexico and maybe even back again.

I wondered how the transmission was done. Probably something like television. Then I wondered why they hadn't done something like that before and then I'd passed the theater and the traffic cops and Hollywood Boulevard opened up like an empty airport runway. I changed lanes back to where I had been then took the next left. Then I realized I'd gone one over so I took the next left and then the next right. With the car now pointed in the right direction I applied pressure to the accelerator and drove into the hills.

As I wound my way to a higher altitude, I saw the Hollywood Sign looming first on my right, and after a few minutes it was more or less dead ahead. It looked big up there on the hill. It sat there almost reluctantly, just waiting for the spotlight to move off it so it could go do something more interesting. As I got closer it seemed to shrink somehow in that way that all landmarks big enough to be seen from afar shrink when you get closer. Then it was gone, hidden by the hills. As I headed toward the mystery address I was surrounded by nothing but winding tarmac and dry scrubby flora that clung to the hills like fluff on a teenager's chin. Above me and the car the sky was very big and very blue.

The road was steep and got steeper. I changed gears and pushed the car upward and wondered where I was going. The view was pretty nice up here. I guessed even movie stars liked to take long drives in the hills now and again to admire it.

The telephone that sat in the cradle between me and the passenger seat rang. I picked it up.

"Having a nice time, Chief?"

Ada always spoke before I could say hello.

"Nice day for a drive, Ada."

"You're right there. Turn left."

I turned left with one hand on the wheel. The narrow winding tarmacked road became a narrow winding dirt road and after a minute there was nothing in the rearview but a brown cloud of dust. Seemed like a strange place to be going.

"What was Charles David doing up here anyway?" I asked.

"Maybe he was taking a hike," said Ada. "People hike. Even actors."

I passed a small sign on a big pole but the sign was covered with dust and I couldn't read it so I kept going. Then the road ended in a big gate and beyond the gate was a building made of corrugated steel, something like a Quonset hut but smaller and with a flat roof. In front of the hut was nothing except a pickup in a surprising shade of lime green. That was all I could see. The road up to the gate was lined with tall brush that obscured the view of anything else.

The gate was closed. It was also locked.

"Dead end," I said.

"Then better bring it back to life," said Ada.

I put the telephone down and left the car running. The padlock on the gate was pretty big and strong but I was bigger and stronger and I broke it without breaking a sweat. Now unlocked, the gate swung open under its own gravity and I walked back to the car and got in it and drove through. I stopped next to the pickup, then saw what was out of the rearview and reversed, swung the car around, and backed up against the hut.

I killed the engine and stepped out, taking a moment to take in the view, which was worthy of quiet appreciation. It looked like half of California was spread out below me, beyond the hills that tumbled down and vanished into a plain as flat as an ocean. I was too far and too high to see any detail, but Hollywood basked in the afternoon sun and that sun caught on windshields and windows and the metal roofs of some buildings, making the whole place sparkle like seaweed washed up on a beach. A little farther, on the left, was downtown Los Angeles proper, a few tall fingers grasping through a reddish haze.

I scanned back to Hollywood and turned down the brightness in my optics and had a little look but I couldn't see my office.

The telephone rang again. I turned back to the car and reached into it and pulled the phone out, stretching the coiled lead out through the door as I stood and kept on drinking in the scene.

I got the first word in this time.

"Ada."

"Wow, Raymondo, what a view, baby!"

I smiled on the inside. "I don't think I've ever heard you so en-thusiastic."

"Hey," she said, "I don't get out much."

"You don't get out ever. And you have no idea what I'm look-ing at."

"Can't a gal use her imagination? I know your location and I know your elevation. The rest is easy, like *that*."

There was a sound like someone snapping their fingers in my ear.

"I'm not sure you can guess what else is up here, Ada."

"So why don't you give me the tour, Chief?"

I switched the phone to my other hand and rested my free arm on the roof of the car. I looked down to my right. The steel hut and its parking lot—if you could call it a parking lot—were on a plateau that was artificial, cut into the hillside. The edge of the pla-teau dropped off fiercely, which allowed the remarkable view. But just over the edge was the top of another structure. It was a series of white panels, elaborately arranged into geometric shapes on the front of wooden telegraph poles and crisscrossed with smaller poles as reinforcement. Even though I couldn't see any more than the top of edge of the structure and even though I was looking at it from behind, it didn't take much detective work to see what it was.

I was standing in a dirt parking lot that overlooked the back of the Hollywood Sign. I said as much to Ada, and then I said, "Seems our movie star was sightseeing."

"Go take a closer look, Chief. Don't worry about the telephone. Nobody is watching."

I felt a little electric surge down my left side. I was supposed to use the phone when I talked to Ada outside the office. I was pro-grammed for it. It was part of the act. Even though Ada talked to me directly inside my mind, Thornton figured it wasn't a good look for a robot to be seen talking to himself in the street.

But that was just the half of it. The telephone might have sounded dead when we called each other, but it wasn't really. I still spoke out loud when I used it but there was a signal howling down the line, a pulse Thornton wove around the frequencies of the standard telephone service, a hidden trick that connected me to Ada directly. That signal took my voice and made it inaudible and undetectable—the perfect scramble, proof against any kind of tapping.

Thornton was a clever man who'd figured that a robot PI and his control computer probably needed a little privacy.

The only thing he hadn't figured out was that the control computer he'd built for me was smarter than he was. In the five years we'd been in business, Ada had made some changes of her own, and not just to me.

Which is to say the telephone in the car was a special kind of telephone, and if I stayed within a certain range of it I could pick up Thornton's secret pulse signal even when the phone was on the hook. The signal was much weaker and the range was lousy, but it was okay.

It still made my circuits ache, but Ada hadn't solved that little bit of programming angst yet.

I glanced back at the hut. There was no sound from it and no movement through the three dusty windows in its side. There was a faint ticking sound, which I put down to the heat of the Hollywood sun shining down on the hut's metal roof.

With not a little effort I hung up the telephone. Somewhere I thought I heard Ada laughing and there was a creak like she was leaning back in the chair behind my desk back at the office.

I moved across the parking lot. The drop at the edge was pretty steep, but to my left there was a track that was still steep but a little better. I headed down it slowly. I slid on the dirt. I looked down the hill. I didn't like the possibilities if I lost my balance.

I frowned on the inside. "If Charles David was sightseeing up here then he had a death wish."

"That gives me an idea," said Ada.

If I had an eyebrow I would have raised it, but I didn't, so I just kept on going down. The path went south and then turned to the right and headed toward the letters. I stopped and looked. I was looking at the *D*. The letters were big and tall and while the angle of the hillside was alarming there was a wide track both in front and behind the letters. Safe enough to take a closer look. I kept up a running commentary for the benefit of a certain computer.

"Wow, they're big," said Ada.

I looked up at the side of the *D*. It was slightly too far away to be towering, exactly, but I still had to look up to see the top.

"Forty-five feet each," I said, doing the trigonometry in my head a couple of times just to be sure.

"Good place for a suicide, then."

I looked around. "Long way to come for it. You'd need to be committed."

"Or a good place to make it *look* like a suicide."

"Oh," I said. I looked back up at the sign and nodded.

"Jump off or get thrown, what's the difference?" said Ada. "By the time you hit the deck nobody is going to know either way."

She had a point.

"Still seems like a lot of work," I said.

"Just let me file it away for future reference. Now keep looking."

I looked. The hillside on the other side of the path was damn steep. It was hard and rough and dusty and covered in rocks and scrub. I didn't particularly feel like falling onto it from the path, let alone from the top of any of the forty-five-foot-tall letters.

It was quiet up on the hill. The breeze had picked up a bit but it didn't carry much on it. High above a jet liner defaced the clear blue sky with a vapor trail that was dirty at the edges.

I moved to the letters, taking the path at the front. I looked up. The letters looked good. In fact, they looked better than good. Fresh paint. No rust. They were made of metal panels. Tin, perhaps. Each was inlaid with light sockets and in each socket was a bulb. I looked out across the rest of the sign. There must have been four thousand bulbs screwed into the hillside. Some of the panels were a little flatter than the others, too. Replacements.

"They've done a good job," said Ada.

I shrugged.

"You don't remember, do you?" she asked.

I shrugged again. "Is that a rhetorical question?"

Ada laughed. It ran through on a loop twice but at the end was something new, like she was taking a drag on a cigarette. I wasn't sure that was part of the recordings that made up her voice or just an echo of something rattling around inside my circuits.

"The sign was falling apart last time I looked," she said.

"When was that, exactly?" I asked.

"I don't remember."

"You and me both then."

"But they've fixed it up. Got it looking nice."

I pondered. I turned and looked at the view and pondered some more.

"The movie premiere," I said. "The big national one." I turned back to the sign. "They were doing up Grauman's Chinese Theatre for it. They must have done up the sign, too. Part of the big show."

"All eyes on Hollywood," said Ada.

"I guess so."

"Wonderful, terrific. The city has done us proud, Ray. Now, keep looking."

I ground something inside my throat. It sounded like someone starting a cement mixer.

"For what?" I asked.

"That's what we're trying to find out, Ray. So how about you quit yakking and start snapping."

I walked around. I looked at the view and I looked at the letters of the Hollywood Sign. I moved around to the back. Each letter had a ladder or two on the back but there was nothing much to stand on once you reached the summit.

I followed Ada's instructions and began taking photographs with my optics. After a few minutes I was onto my second roll of film. I had four packed in my chest.

After a few more minutes I was wondering what the hell I was doing here. The mystery girl had done nothing but left us an address to check out that turned out to be an access road leading to the Hollywood Sign. And that was really a fabulous piece of information because here I was looking at the sign and admiring the view and finding nothing at all.

The dirt around the sign was sandy and it kept my footprints real well, but then I do weigh an imperial ton so most surfaces keep my footprints real well. There were other markings in the dirt, but then I expected there to be. The sign had been renovated sometime in the very recent past and they must have had a lot of people and ladders and equipment up here.

I looked back up at the sign and calculated a few angles for the hell of it, threw in some estimated wind speeds, average body weight, air resistance. Ada was right. The sign had some interesting possibilities.

Then I turned away from the sign and headed down the hillside. Carefully.

5

The hill was steep, but boulders and ruts and the curve of geology made a convenient series of natural steps that spiraled downward. As I made my way down I started noticing the place was littered with bits of wood and metal and glass. Some of the metal and wood was white, some of it was stained orange with rust. The glass was mostly broken, but it was clearly the remains of old light globes. It was the detritus from the sign, left over from the renovation. There was a lot of it.

"Hey, excuse me! Sir? Sir! You can't be here, sir. Sir!"

I turned to my left and there was a guy in blue overalls over a blue denim shirt with a blue denim cap on his head. He was pushing fifty and had a good tan and a beard like Abraham Lincoln. In one hand he held a rake with a long wooden handle. Around his middle was a yellow rope that was slack and traveled somewhere up the hill toward the Hollywood Sign. Balanced in a rut behind him was a big canvas sack that was a deep sea green in color.

I cleared my throat like an old Chrysler in need of an oil change changing gears, and then I said, "Private eye," and I pulled out the wallet with my license in it.

The man made his way to me and I made my way to him. When

we were within fighting distance he peered at the wallet and looked up at my face. He frowned and pushed back his cap a little and made a huffing sound. "That a fact, mister?"

I nodded. "Machines can't lie," I said, lying through my circuits. "I thought I was a 'sir'?"

"Oh," said the man. He kept the frown on his face and pulled the front of his cap down, and then he sniffed and he said, "I'm not sure how it ever worked with you lot. Are you a sir or a mister?" He sniffed again. "Damned if I know. Does it make a difference?" A third sniff. "Anyway, nobody's supposed to be up here without permission. This is all private land. Restricted access. Too dangerous. Even for"—he paused and waved the hand that wasn't holding the rake—"sirs or misters like yourself."

He stood back and leaned on the rake with both hands like a wizard in double denim.

"I've been engaged to find a missing person," I said, hoping this would wipe the frown off the guy's mug, but all it did was add a crinkling of the nose to it. I wondered if I should stop talking in case I turned the guy's face all the way inside out.

The man seemed to be considering something. Whether it was what I had just said or not, it was hard to tell. Then he gave another sniff and half-turned away. He looked at the ground. "You can either help me pick up trash or you can get the hell out. I'll leave that to you."

The man was old enough to remember robots and I had a hunch he hadn't liked them then and he didn't like them—*me*—now.

He stood there, waiting for an answer. I didn't give him one. Instead I looked back up at the sign.

"How many you get," I asked, "jumping off that thing?"

The man shuffled in the dusty soil. When he looked at me he folded his arms over the end of his rake in a way that didn't look at all comfortable. He didn't seem like he wanted to give me an answer and as far as I was concerned that was just fine.

I held up my hands and said "Okay," and then I turned and tried to pick out the path I'd taken down. I took one step and then another, and then the man behind me said, "Fewer than you think."

I turned back around. I was about two feet higher up the hillside than he was and I was another one and half taller than him in the first place. From where I was he looked quite far away.

"Okay," I said.

"But some," he said. He started raking up some trash. Then he stood up and leaned back on the rake and looked up at the sign. I followed his gaze.

"I mean," he said, "you really want to do it, you'll find a way. But don't ask me. I'm just from the Parks Department. The place is locked up at night but there's nobody here. So you want to get in, you could." He paused and looked at me, that frown back and deeper than ever. "You did."

I nodded. No point in arguing.

"You seen many people up here?" I asked.

"Jumpers?"

I shrugged. "Or not."

The man went back to raking. "You get sightseers. They mostly stay out on the road and take pictures. You can get a view from up top. Kids come in, too. Seems a good place for necking I guess. What do I know? They don't cause any problems."

"No vandalism?"

The man laughed and doubled his efforts at raking up the debris. "Maybe once. But they came and done up the sign. Looks as good as new now. Better, even. Those lights haven't worked in, oh, forty years at least."

"When did they fix it up?"

"Oh, they just gone and finished about two days ago. No, three days ago. Took them all of a week. Had a lot of men up here. Lot of men. Hard workers, too. Foreign, see. You want good workers, you get foreign workers."

I didn't know enough about it to venture an opinion so I didn't say anything.

The man kept raking. "Heard them talking," he said. "Yes, I did. Foreign workers. Good sort. Hard workers. You want good workers, you get foreign workers."

"So I've been told," I said. "Shame they didn't clean up after themselves."

The man straightened up and laughed. He took his cap off, took in the view, then put his cap back on. "This mess has been here years. The sign was falling down something real good. None of this is from them. They were good workers. Real clean. Real tidy." He paused. "I think they were Russian. I guess it's real tidy back in the USS of R."

Then the ranger looked at me with narrow eyes. "I guess you're okay."

"I'm okay?"

"You're okay. Have a look around all you want, mister. Just lock the gate on your way out."

I didn't want to tell him that he was going to need a new padlock. "So I'm a mister then?"

The man laughed. "Hell, I don't know. Are robots misters or sirs?" He raked a little then stood tall and leaned on the rake. "Say, did they ever make lady robots?"

I told him I didn't remember and he laughed and shook his head and muttered something to himself. Then he walked to his canvas bag and shoveled crap into it. Then he hoisted it up over a shoulder and moved on. I watched him for a few minutes and saw him stop on another patch of hill where the rubbish from the sign had clumped around some brush. Tucked around his safety rope at the back was a pair of thick gloves that he pulled out and pulled on. They nearly came to his elbows. He bent over and started tugging on a large angled piece of metal with sharp edges.

Hell of a job, cleaning the hillside on his own. But he got on with it and I got on with mine. I took another look back at the sign.

And lo if there wasn't a guy up there, above the sign, standing on what must have been the summit road the man from the Parks Department had talked about. The man was silhouetted against the sky behind him and no matter what I did I couldn't bring the contrast around to make him out, but I could see he was wearing a trench coat and a hat. Tourist, I guessed, stopping to take in the air and the view. I didn't blame him.

The man from the Parks Department grunted, then made a satisfied sigh that you could have heard down on Sunset Boulevard. I looked and saw he had got the metal scrap out of the bush. Then I looked back up at the sign and the man had gone, so I forgot all about him and got back to work.

6

I spent a few hours on that hot hillside but I didn't find anything and I didn't know what I was looking for anyway. There was dirt and there was brush and there was trash and while I could have taken some dirt for spectrographic analysis—being a robot has some uses—I didn't see the point. Charles David certainly wasn't here now and the idea that he'd left something useful, as my client had suggested, was rapidly receding into the realms of fantasy.

Which meant I was at square one. Not even that. Square zero. I started to wonder if Mystery Girl was cracked in the head. The only information she'd given us about the target was a last-known address that turned out to be a hillside high over Hollywood.

I checked around me. Some clouds had materialized high above but they were fighting a losing battle against that infinite blue.

I hadn't seen the man from the Parks Department for a long time, so I thought what the hell and pulled up the collar of my coat and whispered to Ada.

"I got nothing."

"Hands, Raymondo, hands."

I turned on my heel, decreasing my elevation by two inches as I drilled into the dirt.

"So *now* you want me to use a telephone?"

"Someone could be watching."

"There's nobody up here but me."

"What about your ranger friend?"

I looked around one more time. "No clue."

Ada sucked on her cigarette. I stood there and listened. "Okay, time to head home," she said after a moment. "Looks like we're going to need to sit tight on this one. She'll call tomorrow. Maybe we can get something more to chew on then. And if nothing else, she'll want the gold back when we tell her we've come up with a big fat zilch. But it's her own fault."

I nodded to nobody. "Ada giving a refund? Don't tell me you're developing a conscience?"

At that she laughed. A full three loops this time. "Hey, I didn't say we would *give* it to her."

"Someone is going to want that gold back, whether it's Mystery Girl or not."

"Right. And then we can ask *them* a few questions. This thing is starting to stink like week-old fish."

"Okay, I'm coming back," I said. I lowered my collar and adjusted my hat and headed back up toward the sign and the little hut and the parking lot where I had left my car. I'd gone farther than I'd thought and finding the path back up was harder than finding it down.

As I approached the lip of the little plateau I could hear the sound of trash being dumped. Must have been my friend from the Parks Department loading up his Parks Department truck. I kept on climbing and for a moment I wondered what bright-eyed pencil pusher back at the office had decided on eye-popping green as the most suitable livery for their official vehicles. Then I slipped in the dirt and found myself going backward for a foot or two before coming to a graceful halt.

The sound from up ahead stopped. The ranger had heard me. I thought about calling out to say it was me, but as there was no one else on the hill I decided I could save my breath. So to speak.

Then I heard something else. It was that ticking sound again, slow and steady. The sun and the hot tin roof of the hut. It sure was a beautiful day and I bet the man from the Parks Department was looking forward to clocking off the dusty hillside.

I continued my ascent.

When I got to the car the pickup was still there along with the hut, the door of which was open. The man from the Parks Department was rummaging inside for something as the roof over his head ticked and ticked and ticked.

I took the window of opportunity and scooted around the back of the hut. It had been put up close to the embankment that supported the summit road above me, but there was room enough to squeeze in. There were some empty canvas sacks crumpled up and shoved out of sight. Some were covered with dust.

But not all of them.

I picked up the first one, then the second. They were recent additions. I kept digging until I reached the bottom. The soil there was the same yellowish pebble scree that covered the hills.

The soil had been disturbed. It didn't tax my skills of observation to see that there was a small area of dirt that was looser than the surrounds. Someone had been back here. Someone had hidden something.

Someone like Charles David?

I brushed the soil with my foot and about an inch below the surface I saw a black tag that could have been canvas. I reached down and pulled it, and pulled out a metal spike ten inches long and maybe four across. At the end opposite the point was a screw cap with a metal loop for the canvas tag.

I stood up and looked at the spike and turned to head back to the car to give Ada a call. I stopped when I saw the man from the Parks Department standing at the corner of the hut with his hands on his hips.

"You'd better be on your way, mister," he said. "You can't rightly be back here any more than you can be on the hill at all. Say, what's that you got there?"

I walked toward him, holding the spike out. Together we emerged into the sun and stared at the object as it lay across my bronzed steel palms.

The man from the Parks Department swept the cap off his head with one hand, returned that hand to his hip, then peered at the spike with his nose an inch away from it.

"Is that what you were looking for, Detective?"

"Maybe that it is," I said.

"Are you going to open it?" he asked. He stood tall and then when I didn't move he waved his hat at the spike.

I unscrewed the end. It was on pretty tight but when it was off it revealed the spike to be a hollow tube. There were some documents in it.

"Well I'll be . . ." said the man from the Parks Department.

I had even less to say, so I tipped the tube instead. The documents slid out.

They consisted of four photographs and some papers that were folded in three. Letters, maybe.

The photographs were all portraits. Head and shoulders, soft lighting, the subjects posed with shoulders turned just so and gazes carefully directed into the elegant middle distance. The kind of photographs you'd find in a glossy magazine. I didn't know who any of the people were but the man from the Parks Department was able to fill me in and he did so without me even having to ask.

"Hey now," he said and he pointed with a finger covered in dust. "That's Fresco Peterman." The picture to which he was referring showed a thick-necked man with a chiseled jaw and chiseled hair and a smile showing more teeth than an angry shark. The dust from the ranger's finger fell onto Mr. Peterman's charming face. I flicked it off and shuffled to the next one in the deck. A woman, long white hair with a wave to it. Skin smooth as silk.

"Alaska Gray. Boy, she's a looker and no mistake."

Photograph number three. Big eyebrows. A mustache worthy of a police commissioner somewhere on the East Coast where it got cold in the wintertime.

"Erm. Ah." The man from the Parks Department added some dust to his beard as he rubbed it. "Ah. Silverwood? Silverman? Can't remember. Not keen on his pictures. Kinda, y'know."

I looked at the man and he looked at me.

"Y'know," he said. "What's the word I'm looking for? Erm. Ah." Then he clicked his fingers. "Y'know. Boring."

"Oh."

The last image was another man. His hair was curly and too long for my taste, as were his sideburns. They stuck to his cheeks like two furry lamb chops.

"Rico. Rico Spillane. He's funny," said the man from the Parks Department. "Say, what else you got there?"

I unfolded the papers. It was a set of five or six sheets. Invoices of some kind. I didn't follow the numbers but it all looked like bills for food and drink, ordered in bulk. Each page was from a different supplier. All were addressed to the same place.

The man from the Parks Department had stopped talking. He stood there with a frown on his face that was deep enough to send for sleigh dogs and extra supplies.

"The Temple of the Magenta Dragon," I read aloud. "Any ideas?"

My new friend shook his head and rubbed his beard.

"No, no sir. What are these? Stolen, maybe?"

"Could be. Don't rightly know yet."

The man backed away a little and he waved his cap at me.

"Well, look now, I don't much like that idea. This is city land, mister. I think I'm going to need to call my boss, Mr. Overington."

"You don't need to do that," I said. "I'm a licensed PI—"

The man shook his head. I watched as some dust drifted off it and into the sunlight.

"No, no, this needs to be by the book. You can talk to Mr. Overington yourself. You just wait there, mister, I'll call him from the hut. Won't be but a jiffy."

He walked away from me—and quickly, too.

I curled the documents from the tube and slid them into my inside coat pocket, and with the hollow spike in one hand I followed him.

The man from the Parks Department was about to make a telephone call he really shouldn't.

And I'm afraid I had no choice but to stop him.

7

I left the body of the man from the Parks Department in the front seat of his lime-green pickup. Seemed as good a place as any. He would be missed eventually but I bet the farm that the death cert would say "heart attack" or "cardiac arrest." Maybe if the medical examiner doing the autopsy did it well he or she would pick up the signs of something else, but I didn't count on it. The ranger was an older guy carrying a little too much weight doing a hard job under a hot sun.

As I drove back to town I picked up the telephone that sat next to me.

"Hello, Ada," I said.

"You stop to pick flowers?"

"I picked something else, actually." I described the spike and the contents thereof. Ada whistled.

"I'm guessing you know what this all is, then?" I asked.

"What you found is what they call in the business a dead-drop spike. You put your best secrets inside, push the thing into the ground somewhere quiet, and either you pick it up later or you tell your buddies where to go looking."

"What kind of business?"

"The spying kind."

I let that bounce around my transistors for a moment or two.

"Ah, Ray?"

"Still here, Ada. Are you saying that Charles David, the famous movie star, is some kind of spy?"

"I'm not suggesting anything, Chief. I'm just telling you what you found."

"And the papers? What's the Temple of the Magenta Dragon?"

Ada made a cooing sound like she'd just found exactly the right kind of handbag.

"Oh, Ray, Ray, Ray, where have you been hiding?" asked Ada.

If I had an eyebrow to lift I would have lifted it. I didn't feel the need to answer that particular question and Ada came back on the line pretty quickly.

"Sorry. It's only the hottest joint in town, Ray."

"What, a club of some kind?"

"A club of one of a kind. Nobody can get in."

"Something about what you said doesn't quite make sense, Ada."

"No, Ray, listen. The Temple is a nightclub. Everyone who is everyone goes there."

"Even the ones who can't get in?"

"That's the whole point. Nobody can get in unless they are *somebody*."

"Okay."

"Movie stars, producers, directors, agents. The big agents, anyway. But the Temple is where it's at. It's where the rich and famous of this wonderful town go to wet their whistle with no one looking."

"The rich and famous, huh?"

"You betcha."

"Like Charles David."

"Absolutely. Only it looks like he went there for more than a drink and a dance."

"Maybe he wanted some souvenirs."

"Souvenirs that he must have stolen from an office at the Temple, only to hide in a dead-drop spike up on a mountainside, alongside some pictures of his famous friends? I know everyone needs a hobby, Ray, but even famous movie stars aren't that crazy."

"I think I should go to this Temple and take a look around, then."

"Yes," said Ada, "you do that. Hey, your ranger friend. The one who was cleaning up. Did he find the spike, or did you?"

"I did."

"Oh, good."

"But he saw me."

"Not so good. I assume you took care of things?"

"I did."

"Can a girl ask how?"

I explained how. Ada sighed when I was done.

"Seems a shame," she said, "when you had that big sign right there."

"You mean I could have made it look a suicide instead?"

"Sure, why not?"

"Well," I said. "I guess I could have. But I had to be quick. He was about to call up his boss and tell him a robot was up at the sign finding things."

"Fair enough."

I was back in Hollywood traffic now. I said good-bye to Ada and put the telephone receiver back where I had found it.

It was getting late but it was still just a little early for the jet set to get set up at their Temple. I had enough time in my pocket to take a cruise past this magical private club and get the lay of the land and maybe do a little of that old-fashioned surveillance I used to be so good at.

Back when I really had been a detective. Back before Ada took a wrench to my programming and came up with a new and far more profitable business venture.

A metaphorical wrench, I mean.

Because it turned out that Thornton had been *too* good. Ada was programmed to make a profit and whether the professor had meant it to be or not, that program was her prime directive. Thanks to the detective agency, she'd accumulated a lot of contacts—on *both* sides of the law—and in me she had a robot who was big and strong and who could get into places without drawing attention, despite being six feet ten of bronzed steel in a hat.

A robot she could *control*.

See, we were a team. Ada did the thinking and I did the legwork. Which included that surveillance I was so good at, on account of the fact I didn't need to breathe or eat or drink or shift my ass around on the seat to get more comfortable. Stick me in front of a suspicious house and I could watch it all day. Just so long as I was back at the office by midnight, otherwise the memory tape in my chest would run out and I'd be no good for anything anymore.

That's what Ada had said, anyway.

The truth was somewhat different. She'd always told me to be home by midnight because the memory tape in my chest needed to be copied off to a master reel and my batteries needed a recharge. Both of these things took six hours.

Except they didn't. The batteries and the memory tape both lasted a full twenty-four hours and charging up the former and transferring the data from the latter hardly took any time at all. That gave Ada several hours in the smallest part of the day to get to work.

What she had been doing was this: at midnight, she switched the conscious part of my electromatic brain off. And then she gave me new instructions, ones that usually involved sneaking up on people and throwing them out of windows or down stairs or squeezing them in the front seats of pickup trucks, lime green or otherwise. Turns out I had quite the knack.

During the day I was a private detective and during the night I was a private killer and I hadn't even known it.

And I hadn't known it for quite a while. There I was, being all private dick and being good at it, when really all my poking and prodding and questioning and investigating had another purpose, one for a job that only happened at certain hours when the captain was not, shall we say, at the wheel.

But then I found out.

The thing with a magnetic tape system is that the wipes aren't always perfect, no matter how strong the magnet you wipe over them is. Good enough, sure, but never 100 percent proof.

So I started seeing things.

They were afterimages, really—flashes, I called them—of people and places and *jobs*. And the thing was that I really was a pretty good detective, so when I started remembering things I shouldn't have been remembering, I started investigating. Once I started putting things together and seeing a pattern I put things together a little more and then I went to visit Professor Thornton.

I'd identified the problem, and that problem was Ada. A problem, I'd hoped, that Thornton would be able to fix.

Except Ada fixed me first. She let me in on the secret—I guess she felt she had to, as I was about to blow the lid on our new operation to the very man who had created us. Not only did she lay it all out for me, she very kindly came up with one or two little adjustments to my own master program that made me see things the way they really were.

See? A team, I tell you.

And let's just say when I turned up at Thornton's lab the meeting didn't go quite as I had originally planned.

How did I remember any of that? Well, someone starts adjust-

ing your electromatic brain and the computer code it runs, you remember it whether you have a twenty-four-hour memory tape in
your chest or not. The whole kit and caboodle had been flashed into
my permanent store to give me a new primary directive. One that
told me what my new job was.

It was a shame about Professor Thornton, it really was, but
I'd had no choice in the matter. We couldn't let anyone—myself
included—get in the way of our new business plan.

I thought about Thornton quite a lot, and that included the time
it took to unwind my journey down the Hollywood Hills. But I was
soon back in the real world and I let those thoughts float away like
dandelion fluff on a cool evening breeze.

After negotiating more of the heavy traffic no doubt caused by
the commotion around the Chinese Theatre, I found myself on Sunset Boulevard and cruising past a long line of clubs on both sides of
the strip. I kept my optics open and the speed low. There were clubs
for dancing. Clubs for drinking. Clubs for drinking and staring at
dancing girls dressed like peacocks. Clubs for staring at dancing
girls dressed in much less than that.

I don't know what I expected the Temple of the Magenta Dragon
to look like. Something like Grauman's Chinese Theatre, I suppose,
but I only supposed that in retrospect, because what I didn't expect
was the famous temple of high-class pleasure to be a plain black
door sandwiched between a steak house and a building with no
apparent signage.

I parked up and sat in the car and took a good long look.

The door wasn't all black. There was gold on it, in the form of the
numbers 6277 near the top and in the middle a character that looked
Chinese. I wondered what it said, if it said anything. I didn't know
Mandarin or Cantonese and I wondered if the proprietors did. Ada
could look it up, if it was important. I doubted it was but I took a
picture anyway.

The traffic was heavy on the Sunset Strip, and there were a lot of people around. I hunkered down in the car. With a little luck nobody would pay me much attention. I was just a big guy taking a snooze in his car with his hat pulled down low. Real low.

I watched a while but there was no action and the black door of the magenta temple remained very closed and I guessed it would remain in that state for a little while longer. What I really wanted were some facts on the club and its clientele. The documents in the dead drop didn't tell me anything worth a dime. But looking down the street I saw the prime spot for a little homework.

It was an ice cream parlor that looked pretty nice. The front of it was all glass and that glass curved at the corners around the door. But it was what was behind that glass that caught my optic. I zoomed in for a closer look. The view through was distorted by the curve of the windows but I could pick out enough detail to pique my interest.

Inside the ice cream parlor was a mirror that ran the length of the back wall behind the counter. Above that mirror was a row of photographs and they all showed an older man—the proprietor, clearly—in a white cap and apron, standing next to people dressed rather more impressively. There was a scrawl in the empty white space of each of the pictures, which was mostly the man's apron.

They were autographs. The wall of photographs was a wall of fame, a record of the rich celebrities who had popped in for a root beer float before dancing the night away at their private little club just a few doors down.

Right now a tall glass of something cool and creamy sounded like a pretty swell idea, and I didn't even drink.

8

The ice cream parlor was busy, which I thought was a good sign if you were looking for an ice cream, but there was room enough for a one-ton steel man to pull up a stool at the bar in front of the soda fountain. Except I didn't, because the stools were too small and I would have concertinaed it like a bus driving into a cinder-block wall if I had tried to sit down. So I just stood and leaned a little.

On my right were two girls who must have been about sixteen and in front of me was a soda jerk who looked about the same age wearing his white cloth garrison cap with an air of authority I had to admire. He nodded at me, like he saw robots in his joint all the time, and asked me what I wanted.

I considered his adolescent complexion, the skin rubbed clean raw in a hearty but failed attempt to get his acne under control. I wondered on the quality of information I'd be able to pump out of him and lamented the obvious fact that the old guy in the photographs in rank and file on the wall wasn't on duty.

Then I ordered a root beer. When the kid asked if I wanted a float, I said sure, why not. It seemed rude to take up space in his joint—and take up space I certainly did—and not pay the rent before I started asking him questions about the parlor's famous patrons.

The root beer float arrived in a glass worthy enough to be handed to the winner of the Monaco Grand Prix. I said thanks and I paid for it with some of that cash Ada was so fond of, and then I saw the two girls looking, the one nearest out of the corner of her eye like she really wasn't trying to look at all, the other through the bird's nest of the first girl's hair like a Peeping Tom checking out the housewife next door through the garden hedge. I glanced at the kid behind the bar. He seemed to be waiting to see what I did with my float. I pulled the glass toward me. The girls next to me froze and seemed to hold their breath for a very long time.

"Knock yourself out," I said, sliding the giant float across the bar. The two girls looked at the glass and then looked at the soda jerk and then looked at me and the one hiding in the other's hair giggled, trying to stifle it with her hand.

I assumed this was standard operating procedure for teenagers in an ice cream parlor when being given a free drink by a robot so I didn't argue. Then the girls took the float and shared two straws and started sucking. At least they fell into that proportion of the populace who didn't find me too scary to look at.

Same with the soda jerk. Which was good news for me.

It was full dark outside, the Strip lit in shifting curtains of blue and white and red as the neon signs came to life. That light shone on the counter of the ice cream parlor and in the eyes of the soda jerk standing behind it. He had his arms folded now, his lips pursed, just like he was waiting to field my first question. While he waited another teen came out of the back, hat on and apron in the right place. The new jerk could have been the other's twin. They exchanged a look and a nod that didn't need any words to go with it. The new kid looked at me and his gaze stayed there quite a while. Then he got on with serving customers while talking to the two girls next to me, both of whom he seemed much more enthusiastic about.

I played statues with the kid in front of me for a few seconds more, then I nodded up at the row of famous faces that looked down on us both.

"Looks like you get a lot of stars in here to taste the root beer," I said with a smile that only I knew about.

The kid jerked his chin like I was an old pal from the army who had a little hat just like his. "Robots like movies?"

"You bet I do," I said.

This got his interest. He lost the cool, his arms unfolding and a smile moving his bad skin around. He leaned in. "You going to the big premiere, then?" He moved his head a little to one side, but I knew where he meant: Grauman's Chinese Theatre.

"I understand you need to be a certain kind of person to get an invite to the red carpet," I said.

The kid's jaw opened and I saw he was chewing gum. "Come on," he said, "you're the last one, aren't you? Doesn't that make you famous?" Then he stood back and looked me up and down while his jaw moved in the same direction. "Yeah, you'd clean up pretty well. Little oil, little polish. Say, they make tuxes in your size?"

I decided I liked him.

"Not sure I'm the right kind of famous," I said. "May come as a shock, but not everyone likes a robot."

"Ah, that's a shame."

"So who comes in here, anyhow? You get any regulars?" I poked a steel thumb over one shoulder. "I hear they have a club just down the block. This looks like a great place to stop on the way for a glass of milk."

"Oh yeah, oh yeah. Look."

The kid turned and pointed to the photographs. There were musicians, directors, actors, actresses, baseball players, and boxers. There were a couple of football players and a TV game show host and the editor of a big important newspaper from a big important city.

At least that's what the kid said. I didn't recognize any of them except the ones I had pictures of in my jacket pocket.

That is to say, if I'd known who the others were once, I didn't remember them now. Damn that magnetic tape memory.

So I just nodded and went along with it. The kid looked at me over his shoulder and saw me nodding and he cracked a smile wide enough to sail the Atlantic in and then he showed me his back again and kept up with the commentary. He was in his element now and I got the impression that working the fountain was the best job in town.

"And there's Alaska Gray," he said. "Rico Spillane. Parker Silverwood. Fresco Peterman. He was in here just last week he was, was Fresco. Look."

The soda jerk pointed to a picture at the end of the row. Four-for-four, they were the folk whose pictures Charles David had stuffed in a tube and buried up by the Hollywood Sign.

"Fresco's a great guy, great guy," said the kid. "Likes root beer and a float." He looked over his shoulder and gave me the eyebrows. I tried to return the expression but I had no eyebrows to give, so instead I said, "Best floats in town, goes the story."

That might have been true or it might not have been. I had no idea. But the kid waggled his eyebrows and turned back to the wall. He raised his arms like a conductor about to tell his orchestra to put the pedal to the metal and he kept running.

"Bob Thatcher. Millicent Olivier. Charles David—"

Bingo.

"You know his beard is insured for a million bucks?"

That I did not know. But I'd had my first sighting. Not a live one, but now I had two photographs of the missing star. You might even call it a set.

"Oh," said the kid, "and Sheira Shane. Oh boy." He let out a wet whistle at this picture, a black woman with a head shaved nearly to the scalp. She was in a strapless dress and had a long arm draped around the kid's boss and the kid's boss looked pretty pleased with the situation.

"Oh boy," I said, after making a clicking sound that I hoped the kid would take as mutual appreciation of the female form. Then I saw his shoulders drop. "What is it?"

The soda jerk sighed with perhaps a little more theatricality than was strictly necessary, and turned back around.

"Well, mister, they all used to come in here quite a lot. I thought they liked it. But recently . . . well, Fresco was last week like I said, but the others . . ."

"The others?"

"Well, mister, they don't come here so often anymore. I suppose they're busy people, but still, it's a shame. A real shame, it is."

"Oh," I said. "Like Charles David?" I pointed to the photograph. "You could call me a fan. I'd love to get his autograph one day."

The kid's smile came back. "Oh yeah! He's great. Did you see *Blackmailers Don't Shoot*? That movie! Man alive. Charles David is an *artiste*."

I made some more noises the soda jerk seemed to like.

"So when was he last here?"

The kid frowned. "Not for a while. Maybe a month. Busy, right? Actually, I remember. Last time he was here, he was sick in the bathroom. Say, I hope he's okay."

"Stomach flu maybe," I suggested. "Goes around, even movie stars." While I said that I filed away the information about Charles David's movements.

The kid nodded. "I guess." Then he returned to the photographs. After another handful of famous faces he stopped again. He *hrmm*ed but didn't turn around.

"And then there's Chip Rockwell," he said.

I looked at the photograph. It showed a middle-aged man in thick glasses and a checkered sports jacket. He was shaking hands with the old guy in the apron, but he didn't look too happy. Maybe his ice cream had melted.

"He was a great producer," said the boy. "I mean, he made some good pictures. A few great ones, too." He shook his head. "Sad about him. It still cuts me up something fierce."

"Something happened?"

"Yeah, it was big news. Accident. He fell down some stairs."

"Oh," I said, and I left it at that. I wondered if I had had something to do with it, but then people can fall down stairs with or without my help.

Then the kid pointed to the last photo on the row.

"And then there's Eva McLuckie."

He and I seemed to stare at that last picture quite a while. I made another clicking sound, but this time it was my camera taking a snap. I think the kid heard because he turned around and this time his smile wasn't quite so wide. He chewed his lip thoughtfully as he studied something indefinable on the counter in front of him. He reached forward and scratched at the nothing with a thumbnail. Then he adjusted his cap and then he folded his arms again.

I thought I knew the feeling. There was something about seeing Eva McLuckie's face up on the wall that would do that to man and robot alike.

"Shame about her, too," said the kid.

I wasn't really listening. I was too busy looking. Eva McLuckie was really quite something. Small. Might call her petite.

The kid shook his head. "She disappeared. She was filming, oh . . ." The kid winced like he was watching a prizefighter take a dive. Then he clicked his fingers a few times.

Dark hair cut into a bob that was as big as a coal scuttle at the back.

"A movie anyway, something," said the kid. "And she disappeared."

Bangs cutting a razor-straight line above her eyebrows, which
were two sculpted arches above two big eyes ringed in black.

"Zip." The kid clicked his fingers again.

Eva McLuckie, looking like an Egyptian princess.

"Zip, huh?" I asked.

The kid looked me in the optics and nodded.

"Zip. Gone. No trace."

Eva McLuckie, looking a hell of a lot like the Mystery Girl who
had walked into the office with a bag full of gold and an offer I
couldn't refuse.

9

The other soda jerk and his girlfriends were in a deep huddle but I leaned closer to my kid anyway. Seemed my stop for a root beer float was starting to pay off.

"What happened?" I asked.

He shrugged. "Who knows?"

There went that line of inquiry. Maybe the kid behind the bar could sense my deflation because he said, "Apparently she went into her trailer one night and in the morning she wasn't there. That's what I heard, anyway. Nobody at the studio knows where she went. Someone said they were filming all the other parts and they hope she'll turn up to finish the picture. Shame, you know."

"Yeah," I said. "Big shame."

It was starting to feel like I knew something the world didn't.

"She'll miss the party," said the milk boy.

"Ah," I said. I paused. I watched Eva's picture but she wasn't saying much. "What party?"

"The *party*. The red carpet, y'know," said the kid, and he leaned forward until his nose was nearly touching mine. There weren't many people who liked to get so close to a robot.

Well, that close to a robot like me and lived to tell.

"Everyone else will be there," he said. "Fresco. Rico. Alaska. All of them." He shook his head and looked at the invisible spot on the counter again. "Man, it cuts me up, it really does."

Of course. The big premiere. Friday night on the red carpet for *Red Lucky*. I still had a snap of the newspaper article from this morning on file. I brought it up and had a quick re-read.

Red Lucky. Motion picture history, it said. A cross-studio co-production the likes of which had never been made. The article listed the principal cast and that list included Eva McLuckie. Charles David, too. It also included almost everyone who had their mugs plastered over the ice cream parlor wall and a whole lot of people who didn't. I read the list twice and when I was done it looked like me and the milky bar kid here were the only two people in town without a speaking part.

All the major studios cooperating with each other seemed like a pretty big deal. It would take quite a bit of cash money to get everyone temporarily out of their exclusive contracts and working for the competition. The competition that also happened to be co-producers of the motion picture.

Sounded like a real headache to me.

Then again, maybe money wasn't quite the issue it used to be for some people these days. Just look at Eva McLuckie. She had a habit of carrying her bank balance around in gold bars in a fancy athletic bag.

Well. *Somebody's* bank balance.

"I hope she turns up," said the kid.

"Yeah, me too," I said.

And then I said thanks and left a two-dollar tip and headed for the Temple of the Magenta Dragon.

As I walked down the block toward the Temple I contemplated my plan to get in. As plans went it was pretty simple: I was going to walk up to the door and see what happened.

It was a plan, I had to admit, largely dependent on how well disposed the man on the door felt about the fact my face was made of metal. A flash of my detective shield usually did the trick when I had to get in somewhere but chances were the Temple would be a different proposition if it was as exclusive as Ada said it was.

The doorman was there behind a purple velvet rope hanging from two golden stands that were placed on the sidewalk around the club's door. The door was closed. There was no line to get in but there were some peepers hanging around on the street wearing not enough clothes, perhaps ready to throw themselves at their favorite movie star or casting agent should either cross the threshold.

It turned out that the doorman, a gorilla wearing a tuxedo and a permanent scowl, was called Robert and he was a swell guy who thought it was a real pleasure for the club to be entertaining the last robot in the world. Before I even had a chance to pull the shield from my inside pocket he grabbed my hand with one that was about as big and he shook it and then he unclipped the velvet rope and knocked on the black door. The door opened and I turned to Robert with my steel fingers touching the brim of my hat. He saluted in return and then went back to guarding the approaches.

In front of me stretched a black corridor and down that black corridor came the sound of people talking, laughing, drinking, laughing some more, talking some more. Music, too. Something with a beat. All those sounds got louder as I got closer. I kept walking.

And then I was in the Temple of the Magenta Dragon.

The room was large and square and had a low ceiling that was painted a flat matte black, as were all the walls but the far one, which was instead upholstered like a Chesterfield sofa in oxblood leather. The room was dark and smoky, and what light there was came from a blend of white and pink spots that mixed with the smoke to make the Chinese décor pop off the black walls. There were dragons and intricate pierced latticework and some more dragons. The low ceiling was supported by an arcade of pillars that resolved when I got closer into carved bamboo stems that weren't black but a deep jade green. The overall effect was of being outdoors on an ancient Chinese terrace under an ancient Chinese sky on a warm and foggy night.

The so-called Temple was full of people. The servers were Chinese men and Chinese women, the women dressed in black silk wraps with red trim and with their black hair pulled back into buns skewered into place with long black sticks tipped in red, the men dressed in more or less the male equivalent. They balanced trays and skirted the club patrons with an elegance as smooth as the silk they were wearing.

The patrons were another story altogether. They stood in groups and they sat at any number of small round tables that were scattered across the room.

And they were all rich. I could tell that by the clothes, the hair, the jewels, the jewels, and the jewels. The light and smoke reduced the men to pinky-purple ghosts floating in the room, the white of their shirts and their teeth the only really distinguishable features. But the women glittered—what skin that wasn't covered by evening wear slung low in the front as well as the back was covered by pearls and diamonds and other treasures that took that pink and white light and did something special to it before shooting it back at my optics like a laser beam. There were a lot of people in the room but I recognized a large chapter by their photos that hung on the wall of the ice cream parlor just a half block away. Not every member of that parade was here in the Temple. I matched a dozen faces and none of them were Charles David's or Eva McLuckie's.

I walked forward into the club. People parted. People looked at me and laughed but they laughed in that way that spoke of true happiness only found in those who don't need to worry about their retirement. People nodded at me and those nods were appreciative, like they were watching the Mona Lisa stretching her legs around the gallery after hours. I couldn't smile, not on the outside, so I trod carefully as I took a route across the room and tried not to feel like the Queen of England. I was big but people got out of my way. Nobody seemed to mind. In fact, everybody seemed real pleased to see me.

Which I have to admit I liked, before I realized the reason why.

There was no fear or unease in the room because these people—and their *livelihoods*—hadn't been threatened by the robot revolution of the 1950s. These people were rich and famous and no doubt a lot of that wealth and fame was second generation or more—the movie business could run down a family line like hair and eye color. They operated in a rarified atmosphere where they could afford to be curious about a novelty like me. My presence was clearly unexpected but it was also amusing to them, if not downright entertaining. The Temple of the Magenta Dragon was wall-to-wall talent and I was wading neck-deep in the A-list—and for one night only I was part of the crowd.

I reached a table and everyone at it turned to me with big smiles. They looked about ready to burst into applause, so I saved them the trouble and took a left turn and found myself at the bar.

The bar was busy, mostly with waitstaff who were loading up the champagne buckets like it was the only liquid left with which to put out the burning palace. I didn't want to interrupt them to ask for a drink I couldn't drink, so I turned around and watched the crowd and listened to the music.

Some crowd. I matched a few more faces to the photos from the ice cream parlor. I looked at a few more jewels, a few more hairdos, a few more jaws going up and down. The eyes of everyone in the room had left me and returned to conversations and plunging necklines and the bottom of champagne glasses.

Now I got what Ada had been talking about. This wasn't just a nightclub. This was a *temple*. A place of solitude where the biggest cats in Hollywood could just come and be regular people who drank the most expensive liquor in town and wore diamonds like they were cut glass. This was a place you came to enjoy the company of your peers, unmolested by the great unwashed. Everyone here was the same. Everyone here could relax and not worry about being rich and not worry about being famous with the only other people who really understood what that meant.

I started to make a list of who was I going to pump first. The fact that Charles David was a patron, maybe even a regular one, was obvious. The question of how and why he had got a hold of some company accounts was another matter. Someone here—scratch that, *everyone here*—would know him. Who to collar first, I had no idea.

Then someone planted himself next to me at the bar. He was one of the few men not wearing a black dinner jacket. In fact, his dinner jacket seemed to be a green and yellow plaid that under the pink and white lights did something strange to my vertical hold. As I tried to restore the balance in my optics a woman with long white hair and a face thirty years too young for such a color joined the man and he leaned around to kiss her behind the ear. She glanced at the man and then glanced at me and then she headed off to powder her nose or polish her jewels. The man in plaid watched her backside sway away from him. Then he turned to the bar and shook his head at, apparently, himself, before taking a silver cigarette case from inside his plaid monstrosity. He opened the case and took out a cigarette and inserted it into his mouth. And then he stood there with the cigarette sticking out perpendicular to his face like he didn't quite know what to do next.

I knew the man from his photograph at the ice cream parlor. Square-jawed and square-haired with a neck that would make a football lineman weep with envy.

Fresco Peterman.

Seemed I had found my first line of inquiry.

10

I reached forward with my right hand. I extended a finger. If Fresco Peterman saw it coming, he played it cool as a blue spark danced on my fingertip in front of his face. In fact, he even leaned forward a little to touch the end of his cigarette to my improvised lighter. A second later the end was glowing red and the lips around that cigarette pulled back to show me as many of his perfect teeth as possible.

"Hey, thanks, Sparks," Fresco said in a tone that suggested he had his cigarettes lit by the last robot on Earth every day of the week. Without lifting his arms from the bar he sucked on his cigarette and then blew smoke out around it. He nodded at me, then turned back to the bar, then finally brought his hands up into view and rested them on top of it. "Anyone ever put you in a motion picture?" he asked the empty bar space in front of him.

I pursed my lips, or at least it felt like I did. It didn't matter because I didn't have lips and Fresco Peterman wasn't looking anyway.

"No," I said. "As a matter of fact, nobody has yet."

Fresco's shoulders jerked as he laughed and smoked and laughed some more. "I bet you wouldn't have too much trouble learning your lines either, eh, Sparks?"

I helped him laugh and it sounded like a lime green pickup stripping its gears as it tried to get up the Hollywood Hills. "You may have a point there."

Fresco nodded and smoked and nodded again. Then he pulled the cigarette out and turned around to offer me his hand. "Peterman," he said. "Fresco Peterman."

"I thought I recognized the face," I said. I took his hand carefully and shook it. His grip was pretty good. Not as good as Robert's. "It's a pleasure to meet you, Mr. Peterman. Raymond. Raymond Electromatic. I'm honored."

"Electromatic, Electromatic," said Fresco, rolling the surname around his mouth along with a healthy volume of smoke. He nodded and the smoke wafted from the corners of his mouth and from his nose like one of the dragons clinging to the ceiling over our heads. "There's something there, I swear it," he said. "You should talk to my agent sometime. I'll introduce you."

"Well, Mr. Peterman, I wouldn't say no to that." I smiled on the inside, and I thought maybe Fresco could see it, just for a moment, the way he leaned back and relaxed and smiled on the outside.

I relaxed too, although I was careful to lean on the bar only lightly in case I left a robot-shaped dent. Up close the black bar was actually a deep scarlet veneer that really was worth writing home about and I would have hated to see a lug like me scratch it up. I figured if anyone should scratch it, it should be an A-lister. They could afford the repair bill.

Then there was a crackling noise, and I thought for a moment that I really had scratched the bar so I stood upright. Fresco watched me, then smiled, then returned his attention to his cigarette.

The crackling sound kept on going. It sounded like eggs in a pan.

I looked at Fresco but he seemed to be happy smoking and he certainly wasn't frying any eggs I could see.

I looked around. The sound kept on going.

"So what brings you to our little Temple, Sparks?"

I turned to face Fresco. He was leaning on the bar with his elbow now. I looked at his dinner jacket and wondered if I should break the news. I decided not to.

"Business before pleasure, I'm afraid," I said.

"Aren't they one and the same?"

Fresco laughed again and I stood wondering what he varnished his hair with. He puffed hard enough on his cigarette to send a message to Canada and then he clicked his fingers. A woman appeared out of the smoke. She was standing behind the bar and maybe she had always been there. She was Chinese like all the staff seemed to be, but unlike the servers canvassing the room she had her long hair straight down and when she turned around to fill Fresco's order I saw the back of her silk dress was missing. She had a tattoo of a dragon curling down her spine.

Then she turned back around and moved three long, thin glasses of fizzy wine onto the bar. Fresco nodded but didn't say thanks and he didn't swap the glasses for any money, either. The woman faded away and the movie star pushed a glass toward me. I said thanks and took it and held it by the thin stem. Fresco finished half of his in a single gulp and didn't say anything when I didn't do the same.

"Truth is, Mr. Peterman," I said, "is that I'm here looking for someone." I paused and changed my mind. "Actually, a couple of people."

"Looking?"

"I'm a private eye, as a matter of fact."

"No trouble I hope, Sparks?"

"Can't say."

The smile that darted around Fresco's thin lips was playful and furtive at the same time. I figured that if you put that smile up on a silver screen say sixty to seventy feet across and half that high you could make a lot of women swoon and make a lot of money in the process.

Whatever it took to make it in this town, Fresco Peterman had it. Even in a plaid dinner jacket you could see from the moon, he had it.

"Can't say or won't say?" said Fresco, and he said it somewhere on the road between an accusation and a weary but wry question. It was like he was reading from a script, feeling out the emotions and the tone and the voice of the character he was playing. Maybe he wasn't so happy to chat now he knew I was a detective.

"Can't," I said, ad-libbing as fast as my circuits could manage. "I'm hoping they're okay, but you never know."

"They?"

The crackling sound was still there. I wondered what the hell it was. Nobody else seemed to be bothered by it and it was so faint it surely couldn't be heard over the hubbub of the club anyway. Must have been a bug in my audio. I glanced around the bar, looking for a phone. I didn't have much time before I had to head back to the office but I thought I should probably dial in and say hello to the boss.

I turned back to Fresco. He still had that smile on his lips and his cigarette didn't seem to be burning any lower. Now that's what I call acting.

"They?" he asked again, like I was an actor in need of a prompt.

"You know Charles David, I expect. Eva McLuckie, too?" I asked.

Fresco barked a laugh. It was staccato and loud but while it bounced against the noise of the club, no problem, it didn't quite reach his eyes.

I rolled my neck, in case that crackling was cellophane stuck in my collar from the dry cleaner's. It wasn't.

"Charles is a great friend, Sparks, and Eva is quite something let me tell you." He said it like he had no idea who I was talking about and couldn't have cared less. Then he drained his fizzy wine and went looking around the bar for another.

"Say, is Mr. David here tonight?" I asked. "You could call me a fan."

"Ray, you're a fan."

"Ah, yes, that's good," I said. "But is he here? Seems like everyone else from *Red Lucky* is." I waved a big steel hand in the general direction of "everyone."

"Oh, hey," said Fresco, suddenly animated, sliding closer and nudging me with an elbow. "You're coming to the premiere, of course?"

"Well, I—"

"No, look, I insist. No, no, you'll be my guest. I insist. It'll be great, Sparks, trust me. It'll be great."

I nodded. "Well, thanks," I said, and I wondered what Ada would say to a night off. Then I quit wondering and started steering my new celebrity buddy back around to the topic at hand.

"So is he—"

"Who, Chuck? I don't think he's here. Not tonight. Haven't seen him in a while."

"Okay. How about Ms. McLuckie?"

"You sure there's no trouble, Sparks?"

"Well, like I said, I'm not at liberty to discuss matters. But let's just say there are some concerned parties involved."

"Oh she's fine, fine," said Fresco. He said it like he had no idea what I was talking about.

"But she's not here either?"

Fresco's eyes narrowed like he was thinking very hard about the question. He reached inside the construction he thought was a dinner jacket and pulled the cigarette case out again. He took out a

cigarette and replaced the case inside the jacket. Then he reached
into the other side and took out another case. It was also silver but
it was smaller, like a box for matches. He kept his narrow eyes on
me as he flipped the lid of the box, took out a single small white
round pill from among the other small white round pills inside, and
put it in his mouth. He snapped the box shut with a little more force
than seemed really necessary, pocketed the box, then used the last
swirl of champagne in his dead glass to get the small pill down his
throat.

Then he put the glass down and he said, "No, she isn't here." Then
he looked around the bar again. "What do I have to do to get some
service?" he asked nobody in particular, but when he snapped his
fingers the lady behind the bar with the dragon tattoo materialized
and refreshed his drink. I thought that kind of service was actually
pretty good.

"I heard she walked out of a picture," I said.

Fresco gulped his fizzy wine and when he came up for air he
gasped like he'd just taken a long, cool draught from a Scandina-
vian mountain spring. He fixed me with his eyes again. They were
still narrow. Maybe a bit hard now, too.

"She's fine. Resting. Nervous exhaustion, you know. It's a tough
job we have."

I looked at the half-empty glass in Fresco's hand and then I looked
around the smoky interior of the Temple of the Magenta Dragon
and the jewels that glinted in the dark like the span of the Milky
Way and I thought, yeah, it's a tough job you have.

"And the walkout?"

Fresco finished his drink and pressed the empty glass into the
bar top. Then the smile flickered, once, twice, then reignited as the
movie star barked another one of his short, harsh laughs. He shook
his head.

"I'm sorry, Sparks. I shouldn't be like that. Not with a swell guy like you. No, that part isn't true. Where'd you read it? The *Daily News*?"

I didn't commit one way or the other. Fresco shook his head again. He put his new cigarette between his lips but rather than wait for my parlor trick he reached over the bar and grabbed a flat book of matches from a small collection of the same.

"The *Daily News*," he said with a shake of the head and a flick of the wrist as his cigarette caught fire. "Those asinine pinheads. They don't know jack, Sparks. If I were me I'd throw them off the Holly-wood Sign, the whole lot."

I didn't say anything in reply but I did think that was an interest-ing statement to make.

Then his silver-haired companion reappeared at his side, curling one arm up to his shoulder, and touched her lips to a spot of skin somewhere behind Fresco's right ear. They talked with some ani-mation in low voices but I was distracted by something else.

That crackling had gotten louder. A lot louder.

Then I blinked, or at least it felt like I did, and I saw Fresco's glam-orous friend was looking at me with cool blue eyes. Her hair glowed pink in the lights of the club.

"Sparks," said Fresco, the playboy demeanor back and turned up to eleven, "I'd like you to meet a very great friend of mine, Ms. Alaska Gray."

I gave a small nod.

"Alaska," said Fresco, cigarette in hand as he gestured at me like a landscape gardener pointing out a particularly fine specimen of tall pine, "what you see before you is an example of the pinnacle of human achievement, a wonder of the modern age—hell, a wonder of *any* damn age at all. Because this fine fellow is, in fact, the very last robot in the world, one Mr. Raymond Electromatic."

Alaska's eyebrow went up and she held out her hand and turned her head in a way I would have said was alluring. I took the hand as gently as I could but while I knew the protocol I didn't bother with a kiss. I didn't have any lips and I figured my bronzed steel face was a probably a little cold to the touch anyway.

Alaska took a breath and seemed to hold it. She looked sideways at Fresco. "And you know him as . . . Sparks?" she asked. She'd let the breath out first.

Fresco laughed and adjusted his cigarette and nudged me with that loose elbow again. "Go on, Sparks, give her the show."

I lifted my hand, palm up, fingers curled like I was ready to catch a falling apple. Then I deliberately shorted a solenoid and let the little excess charge leak through my fingertips.

And as I watched Alaska watch the blue arcs jump from finger to finger with wide-eyed delight with Fresco rocking back on his heels with laughter, I listened to the crackling sound and realized just what the hell it was.

I needed to talk to Ada, and quick.

I closed my hand. Show over.

Fresco recovered himself and patted the front of his plaid jacket like he was checking it was still there. Sadly it was.

Alaska raised a tall glass that had appeared in her hand and gave me a salute. "I'm impressed, Mr. Electromatic."

Fresco leaned back into Alaska as he looked at me. "I was just saying, my dear, that Sparks here should be in the movies."

The crackling sound ran on and on and on. I started taking readings.

"You know," said Fresco. "Science fiction. He'd fit right in, right?"

"Oh, science fiction! It's a scream!" said Alaska, doing her best impression of surprise at winning an Oscar by placing her free hand on her chest and leaning back like a ladder was about to fall on her. "It's all Aldebaran and pink pretzels and the fourth moon had already risen, right?"

I didn't know anything about pretzels and why they would be

pink, but right now I had other things to worry about. Like why that nervous exhaustion Eva McLuckie had so sadly come down with hadn't prevented her from walking into my office with a bag of gold. Like how a strange chase up to the Hollywood Sign had led me to the Temple of the Magenta Dragon.

Like how one movie star had apparently taken out a contract on the life of another.

Like how Fresco Peterman and Alaska Gray laughed and drank and smoked and while they did those things they crackled like kids at camp eating graham crackers under the bedsheets.

I took another reading from my Geiger counter. Fifty-seven rads were wafting off Fresco. Nearly eighty off Alaska. These two were the hottest stars in Hollywood.

Literally.

I left them laughing and drinking and smoking and radiating and headed for the telephone at the end of the bar.

11

"I can't believe it," said Ada inside my head as I held the telephone to my ear. The roar of the club behind me didn't have any impact on our private conversation.

"They're radioactive. Cooked medium rare, by my calculation."

"I mean," said Ada, "what the hell kind of name is Fresco? First name Al, by any chance?"

I simulated a frown. "Um. Fresco is his first name. Fresco Peterman. Are you listening to me, Ada?"

"I'm all ears, Raymondo. So, those movie stars are hot, and not just on the silver screen. What are you going to do about it?"

I checked the time. It was running out faster than I thought. Pretty soon my batteries would be empty and my memory tape full. That didn't sound like much fun.

"I'll talk to some more people. Maybe take a look around a little. Both Charles David and Eva McLuckie are apparently out of the picture—"

"Very good, Ray."

"Pun *not* intentional, but this is their crowd. Fresco knew a little. Maybe someone else will know a lot. Funny, isn't it?"

"Hilarious," said Ada. "What is?"

"How one movie star would take out a contract to kill another. I've heard of professional jealousy, but this seems a bit dramatic."

"You're doing it again, Ray."

"Ah, oh."

"But," she said, "you're right. If Eva is behind the contract at all."

"The gold. I remember."

"Right. So go take a look around. Ask some questions. But don't make me wait up, Raymond. I need you back here by curfew."

"I got it."

I put the phone down and thought things over and then I turned around to face the room and I thought things over some more. Fresco hadn't said much that was useful and really the most interesting thing about him was his taste in clothes and the little personal problem he had with radioactivity. His lady friend, too. They'd both been exposed to something, maybe for a long time given the amount of energy rising off of them.

But did that have anything to do with the absence of Charles David? It was hard to see any connection but my case felt a little kooky. Fresco and Alaska's radioactivity certainly was. Seemed worth a bet to keep one bit of weirdness in mind as I investigated the other. But in the meantime I needed to find something out soon so I could give the lovely and nervously exhausted Eva McLuckie her report tomorrow.

Well, Ada would give her the report. I wouldn't remember the club or the movie stars or the ice cream parlor or the man from the Parks Department. Ada would. I had a feeling we were in for a long chat in the morning as she filled me in.

As I lamented this state of affairs I noticed something had changed in the Temple of the Magenta Dragon. The music was still tripping a fast beat and the place was still filled with smoke and the silk-clad servers doing the quickstep around the patrons.

But I couldn't see Fresco Peterman or Alaska Gray.

Then I couldn't see Sheira Shane or Millicent Olivier. I couldn't see Parker Silverwood or Bob Thatcher or Rico Spillane.

I couldn't see any of the big names I recognized from the ice cream parade. And there were plenty more missing who I couldn't name either.

The ticking of my Geiger counter had slowed to a bored and dis-interested tapping in the back of my electromatic brain. In fact, the level of radioactivity in the club was now lower than it had been when I'd first walked in.

I put two and two together and didn't like the answer. Because while the joint was still jumping what I had left in front of me was now the B-list. The big stars had gone, leaving lesser actors, directors you thought you knew but couldn't list any of the pictures they'd made, producers who controlled big checkbooks but were name-checked not in the *Daily News* but in industry magazines that gathered dust in the waiting rooms of casting agents, some of whom were still in the room, too.

This being Hollywood there was still a lot of glitz on show, but it was tarnished beauty. Sure, there was still an electricity in the air. But what there wasn't was any radioactivity.

I felt a pressing need to ask Fresco and Alaska and the others a whole lot of questions, so I did what every robot assassin who used to be a private detective would do in this situation.

I went to look for them.

12

Nobody stopped me. The staff were all too busy running the four-minute mile with trays of drinks and buckets of ice and by the time I'd walked through enough back doors and walked down enough back corridors there weren't any staff left to bother me anyway. The pink and white lights were still there, though, lighting the whole damn building like a sinking submarine. And I knew my own air was starting to run out.

I walked on. I followed my nose because, like money, radioactivity had a distinct smell, only one measured in rads. I turned the counter up and it ticked in my ear like someone treading broken glass. I kept on walking and that dangerous crackle got louder and faster as I walked.

The Temple of the Magenta Dragon was a big place behind the scenes. In fact, the club itself seemed tiny compared to backstage, which was a labyrinth of brick corridors painted black. The Chinese décor was gone. I thought that was a shame. I had a sudden urge to have a dragon or two on my side.

I reached some stairs. My nose led me down so down I went. There was a door at the bottom and from the other side I could hear people talking. They sounded about as far away as the moon so I quietly opened the door and quietly moved myself to the other side of it. Then I closed it behind me without a sound.

I was at the top of more stairs. There was no handrail and the air felt damp. I thought some more about submarines as I descended, but at least the pinkish light had gone now. The stairs were black brick and covered in darkness as thick as the cigarette smoke in the club somewhere above me. The room below was lit in a weak and yellowish light. I kept close to the wall, where the shadows were deep enough to take a bath in, and down I went.

The basement under the club was damp and dirty. The ceiling was low, and like in the club above, supported by rows of columns. Unlike those, the columns here were plain brick painted black. In the dim light of the basement these columns provided long shadows that could have been tailor-made for a robot like me to hide in. As I crept forward the Geiger counter in my head started up with a jazz solo so I cooled it off just to hear myself think a little.

They were gathered around a big round table, on top of which was a big square red cloth covered with embroidery in metallic gold and black, clearly borrowed from the more salubrious establishment upstairs. The yellow light came from a big bare globe that hung in a wire cage from the ceiling. Despite the bulb's size, it wasn't doing much of a job and the darkness beyond the table was pretty thick.

And by *they,* I meant the A-listers. They were all here, some sitting around the round table and some standing. The evening wear, the dresses and suits and jewels, they were all covered by shapeless smocks, high at the neck, tied at the small of the back like something a surgeon might wear except for the fact the coverings were black as pitch.

That wasn't all that was new.

Every man and woman in the basement wore thick rubber gloves that went right to the elbow, and everyone wore dark glasses, each pair large and rectangular and the same as all the others.

All those shaded eyes stared at the man at the head of the table. Unlike the others he was wearing a black dinner jacket, a white shirt, and a black tie. His face was nothing but a pair of those dark glasses stuck onto a ball of white bandages that made a tight orbit of his entire head. The tuxedoed mummy sat with his arms out of sight on a chair that was too low, making the big round table cut him high on the chest.

Must have been a hell of an accident.

Nobody spoke. Nobody moved. Everyone was waiting for something. What, I had no idea, but it couldn't have been for the Mummy to say anything because the Mummy's mouth had a tight swath of gauze sweeping right over it. The poor guy couldn't speak even if he wanted to.

My time was nearly up. As fascinating as this freak show was I had to think about getting out of there before I turned into a pumpkin.

And then she stepped right out of those shadows and into the light of that big bulb. She was in a black smock and she had the glasses and the rubber gloves. The glasses were a little too big for her small face with its pointed chin.

Eva McLuckie walked toward the table. The A-listers watched her and made room and I wondered what the hell kind of Hollywood party this was. Hell of a time to be rehearsing a play.

As she approached the table my Geiger counter went into overdrive.

The girl was glowing like a blast furnace.

Looking around at the others, she said, "Report," but it took me a moment to process, because when she opened her mouth the voice that came out wasn't the one I remembered from that morning. It was lower in tone and the consonants were clipped in a way that just wasn't American, the r's rolling like oil on a hot griddle.

Alaska Gray: "All are in position."

"Stability?"

Parker Silverwood: "Stability achieved to ninety-nine percent."

The voices. The accents. All coming out of the mouths of movie stars and all sounding like they were on the wrong side of the Iron Curtain.

"Conditional readiness?" asked Eva.

Fresco Peterman: "Phase three ready."

"Additional?"

Alaska Gray: "Additional, phase four. Prepared and on standby."

"Initiate phase four."

Alaska Gray nodded. "Contact will be established."

Eva paused. Then she nodded. "Report accepted. We are close now to the final part of the program."

I didn't like the sound of that.

"Comrades," said Eva in her weird voice, "you have all conducted your operations with maximum efficiency. When the program is complete, you will all make fine additions to the Supreme Council of the Western Hemisphere."

Now, maybe it's just me, but when people start talking about Western Hemispheres and Supreme Councils I get a little nervous.

There was a period of silence, six and seven-tenths seconds, according to my chronometer, when nobody moved or spoke. Some meeting. Those around the table I could see clearly were smiling. Fresco Peterman was smiling so much his cheeks pushed his big glasses up so high I wasn't even sure he could see out of them properly. All the while, the bandage-wrapped Mummy at the head of the table sat perfectly still and perfectly silent.

Then someone cleared his throat. The chairs creaked and feet shuffled as everyone turned to look at the culprit.

Rico Spillane wasn't smiling. He was wearing the glasses like everyone else and they were wrapped around sideburns you could

carpet a small parlor with. He seemed to shiver and I saw those sideburns were flecked with moisture, like morning dew on a hedgerow.

"Ah," he said. Then he coughed a little again. "Phase four . . .
phase four." He spoke in the clipped tones of Eastern Europe, like
everyone else in the room who had spoken.

The only part of Eva McLuckie that moved was her head, and she
turned it sideways to look at Rico Spillane in a way that would have
made my skin crawl if I had any.

There was something in the air. Something new, something other
than radioactivity.

Anger. Behind those big glasses, Eva McLuckie was not happy
with the interruption.

Rico Spillane looked around the table. He turned his head
slowly, like he was taking in the scene, and then he turned his head
quickly, like he wasn't really sure what was going on.

I knew the feeling.

Then his mouth opened and his jaw went up and down and when
he finally found his voice it was his own, the accent as American as
apple pie and Mutually Assured Destruction.

"What . . . what's going on? Where am I?" Then he saw the
Mummy sitting at the end of the table and Rico recoiled, pulling
one arm up to shield his face. "What the hell is going on? What the
hell is that?"

I watched as that raised arm knocked against the big glasses Rico
was wearing. He jumped, then pulled them off, and stood there staring at them with eyes that I could now see were wide with fear and
confusion.

While Rico had his little nervous breakdown, everyone else was
as still as I was. Nobody spoke. It was hard to see what was going
on with the stack of black brick in front of me, but I couldn't risk
getting any closer. The basement was dark but maybe it wasn't *that*

dark and while I figured I could reverse and leave without being
seen, I didn't much feel like trying my luck with anything else.

More dead air. Three seconds. Four and a quarter.

Everyone was watching Rico Spillane. Myself included.

He stumbled forward and leaned on the table.

Eva McLuckie's frown deepened. "Report, Comrade," she said.
And then she said what sounded like "*Otchet!*" but I couldn't tell. I
didn't recognize the language. Was it Russian? Maybe it was. It went
rather well with the accents.

Then Rico groaned. He raised a hand and rubbed his forehead
and he stumbled backward. The people behind him got out of the
way. He stepped outside of the glow of the big bare bulb and seemed
to vanish into the shadows. From the darkness he kept muttering
his new mantra, each iteration colored more and more with rising
notes of panic.

"What the hell is this? What the hell is this? What the hell is this?"

"COMRADE."

The voice that came from under those bandages sounded just like
the kind of voice that you'd expect to come from a mummy. It was
as dry and as dusty as the dirt under the Hollywood Sign and buzzed
and clicked like the Geiger counter in my head had picked a fight
with a hive of angry bees.

Rico stumbled back into the light and then every part of him
froze in place except his lips, which continued to form the five-
word repeat even though his vocal cords had stopped cooperating.
He stared at the Mummy with eyes as round as quarter dollars.

"COMRADE SPILLANE HAS BECOME DISCONNECTED," said the
Mummy. "COMRADE SPILLANE MUST BE REPROCESSED IMMEDI-
ATELY."

Parker Silverwood and my old pal Fresco Peterman grabbed Rico.
Rico struggled against them but it was only a token effort and after

a moment he gave up altogether and just hung there, his toes touching the floor

I didn't move and I didn't breathe. Two relatively easy things for a machine to do, but I hoped it was enough.

The pair dragged Rico around to the head of the table.

"RETURN HIM TO THE CENTER FOR RE-TRANSFER," said the Mummy.

Eva McLuckie turned and nodded at the Mummy.

"At once, Mr. Rockwell," she said.

Then she turned back to the others and clicked her fingers at Parker and Fresco before disappearing into the dark of the basement. The two men followed, Rico dragged between them. Everyone else at the table looked at each other and looked at the Mummy, but nobody said anything.

It was time for me to go. Re-transfer didn't sound like too much fun and something was up with Rico Spillane, but I could hardly go in and help even if I wanted to. My batteries were low and my memory was getting full and I already had plenty to think about.

Like what a bunch of radioactive movie stars were doing in a basement of a club, talking in Russian accents, dressed up in some kind of protective gear while they had a secret meeting of what looked like the Hollywood Communist Party. Like what the missing movie star Eva McLuckie—my *client*—was doing in the middle of it all.

Like what dead movie producer Chip Rockwell was doing alive, if not exactly well, giving orders to his comrades in a voice that made me want to scratch my fingers down a blackboard just to get it out of my head.

I turned to leave.

And then my alarm went off and I woke up to another beautiful morning in Los Angeles.

13

I woke up and stretched inside my mind—a tic from Thornton's template, given I had nothing in particular to stretch—and looked around the computer room. Ada was all around me, her circuits clicking like a Cadillac cooling in an evening breeze.

There was a newspaper sitting on the table in front of me. First edition, Wednesday, August 11. That was normal. What wasn't normal was the fact that it was alone. Although I had no specific memory of it, I was sure my hat usually kept it company. And what in turn kept my hat company was my jacket, which should have been on the back of the chair.

Something wasn't right, although I had no empirical data to go on. It was just a hunch. A feeling somewhere in the diodes down my left side.

I glanced down. My chest door was open and the cables were plugged in. Then I saw that my jacket and hat weren't the only items of clothing missing. Gone too were my shirt and tie, pants, underwear, shoes, socks, the lot. I was as naked as the day I was built, six feet ten of bronzed steel and nothing else.

That wasn't necessarily a problem. I was a machine, after all. The clothes were an afterthought but I liked suits and hats and shoes (especially shoes) and I wore them because it made me feel more . . . normal.

I looked up and into the winking and blinking lights of the console on my right.

"Everything at the cleaners today, Ada?"

Ada hadn't said anything yet, but before she spoke there was a pause like she was dragging on her fifth cigarette of the morning.

"If you want to think of it like that, knock yourself out."

"If I want to think of what like what, Ada? Shouldn't I be wearing a suit?"

"Like every self-respecting button man, Chief."

"So what gives?"

I unplugged and stepped out of the alcove and moved to the table and looked at the paper. I wondered who delivered it. Maybe it wasn't delivered. I supposed the first edition was probably on sale before midnight and I supposed there was a newspaper box on the corner outside the office. The person who delivered the paper to the table in the computer room was probably me, making sure I had a chance to catch up on the world around me as soon as I got out of bed. A small but vital effort in compensating for the fact that I couldn't remember yesterday at all.

"So many questions, so little time, Ray," said Ada. "Now quit yakking, I'm reading."

"Don't tell me—Agatha Christie?"

Ada laughed and there was a clinking like she was stirring the creamer into her first coffee of the morning. A moment later that image had gone. "Actually, the effects of ionizing radiation on human tissue, as a matter of fact."

"Sounds like a wheeze."

"I have some bad news to break to you."

"Spill."

"Don't you want to sit down first?"

"Ada."

"I heard that bad news is best heard with the knees bent."

"The more you dawdle the more I rust, Ada."

"Okay, Chief," she said. "You had a little accident."

"Oh?" I paused and started an internal diagnostic. The universe had been created four minutes ago and everything felt real swell, but I didn't like Ada's tone.

"Yeah," said the boss. "I'm afraid to say you won't see that suit again. Your hat, either."

"Oh." I liked that hat.

"There's another suit and shirt and tie and hat in the closet."

So I said thanks and went over to it. It looked like a tall white cabinet like the other tall white cabinets in the room, and when I opened it I found it had a dozen suits in brown and yellow pinstripe and three long trench coats in tan and two hats and a bunch of folded shirts and rolled ties. I had no idea I kept such a gentleman's wardrobe. There was a drawer at the bottom that had five pairs of black shoes lined up in a neat row.

"Oh," I said again, and Ada laughed while I got dressed, but at least when I was dressed I felt myself again so I turned back around and watched the tapes spin and the lights flash and I asked the obvious question.

"So what happened to the suit? What kind of accident did I have? Road traffic?"

"Nuclear," said Ada. "You were so hot I had to send your clothes to the bottom of the ocean in a lead casket."

I gave my diagnostic subroutine the hurry-up. Maybe Ada sensed something because she laughed again.

"Don't get in a sweat, Chief," she said. "You're fine."

"It wasn't a power leak? Batteries okay?"

"Not a power leak. Your chassis is sealed tighter than my purse."

Coming from her I took that as a compliment. But it was a relief,

anyway. I put the diagnostics on the back burner and stood there
in the computer room like a statue for a while. Ada didn't speak.
The clock above the door that led to the outer office ticked away
toward oblivion. Outside the window the sun was casting long
shadows on the rough brick of the building opposite. I glanced at
the paper and thought about picking it up to read and then I thought
twice.

"Something on your mind, Chief?"

"I was just thinking," I said.

"So I gathered."

"No, I mean, I was just thinking. You know that the color magenta
isn't part of the visible spectrum of light?"

"You learn something new every day."

"Me particularly."

I thought about the color magenta. I thought about the color gold.
I thought about Egyptian princesses.

I don't know why I thought about these things, but I did. They
were fragments. Abstract ideas floating around in my circuits.
Something from yesterday, probably. The more I thought about
these things the more they faded away.

After a few minutes of chasing echoes around my circuits I
cleared my throat, or I pretended to. It sounded like the clutch in
my Buick slipping and this got Ada's attention.

"Don't worry about it, Chief," she said.

"I'm not," I said, and I wondered if that were true or not. "I'm
guessing we had a job yesterday."

"That we did."

"One that had me juggling plutonium."

"You know, you might not be too far from the truth there, Raymondo."

I glanced down at the newspaper. Kennedy was in Cuba and
there was a special film premiere on Friday. Special enough to be

front-page news, with a photo of a guy in dark glasses and a carved block of wood on his head that I took to be his hair and very poor taste in clothes. His picture was bigger than the president's.

That's Hollywood for you.

"Anything I should know about yesterday?" I asked, my eyes back on the spinning tapes and flashing lights. Some of the tapes stopped spinning and reversed at top speed. I didn't like it when that happened. Ada wasn't telling me something.

"Don't worry about it, Ray."

"I'm not even sure what there is to be worried about. Do you need me back on the job or what?"

"We'll need to talk about that later, Chief. In the meantime, we have a new number."

I shrugged, on the inside anyway. This was how it worked. Ada ran the show and I did the heavy lifting. She could remember yesterday and I couldn't. So all I could do was trust her and do what she said. Today was a new day and there was a new job.

There was a printer to my right, underneath one of the consoles. It began spitting out a continuous sheet of perforated paper. It sounded like a sewing machine on overdrive.

I walked over and picked up the edge of the paper and slid it through my fingers as I read the information coming out of the wall. The letters were big and black, all capitals.

A name. An address. A number.

The address was the Ritz-Beverly Hotel. It was on Sunset Boulevard. That didn't bother me. It wasn't far to go.

The number I took to be a room somewhere in the hotel. So far, so good.

The name I didn't recognize and there was the rub. I thought I should. I tried again but came back with a handful of nothing. If I had known it, I didn't now. Maybe I never had. Maybe it was just an echo of Thornton's template stuck between a solenoid and a silicon chip. Because with his personality and mannerisms came his memories. Not all of them and not memories exactly. But impressions, ideas, notions that were vague and smoky.

Maybe Thornton had known a person called Eva McLuckie.

I looked up and picked a point where the wall met the ceiling. There were no electronic eyes in the computer room but I knew Ada could see me.

"New target," I said.

Ada said nothing.

I looked down at the paper in my hand. My eyes were drawn back to the name, no matter where else I pointed them. While I fought with my optics another printer began churning. There was a long slot in the computer bank above the ticker-tape machine. Photographic printer. We didn't always get pictures, but they were useful when we did. I didn't know how Ada got our clients. Contacts made while we were a detective agency, probably. You meet all kinds in that line of work.

But that wasn't my department. My department was walking out the door and doing the job. Today, seemed like I had a little help.

The churning stopped and a photograph flopped out of the printer and into the catch tray like a disappointed man falling into an empty bed. The picture was facedown. I reached for it.

"I don't like this," said Ada when my hand was halfway home.

"What's wrong?"

Ada was silent. Maybe she was thinking things over. I read the info sheet again. Then I looked up. "Ada?"

Then I thought again about the color magenta, and when I thought about gold this time it wasn't the color but the metal.

It was something from yesterday.

Ada seemed to sigh, or maybe I just thought she did. Somewhere in the afterimage of a memory an older woman pulled her legs up off the desk in the front office and tucked her skirt down a little as she turned to look out the big window as stormy weather approached.

I didn't like that imagery much so I forgot about it and reached for the photo and picked it up and turned it over and held it up so I could get a good look.

"Wait a minute, Ray," said Ada. "Cool it a little."

I looked at the photograph and I had a sinking feeling somewhere between my voltage converter and neutron flow reversal coil.

"You know who this is, don't you, Ada?"

"You too, Chief," she said.

"So you going to lay it out for me or not?"

"Quiet, Raymondo. I'm thinking."

"Okay," I said. I curled the photo and slipped it into my jacket. Then I grabbed one of the new hats from the closet. I was ready to roll. All I needed was the word from Ada.

I stood there with my hat in my hand for quite a while. To make a change I put the hat on and stood there some more. I looked around the room for nothing in particular. My hat suddenly felt like it didn't fit so I took it off and checked the label inside. I assumed this number was the same size as the old one so I put it back on. It didn't feel any better.

Ada's tapes chattered and lights flashed. She wasn't talking. I didn't like it.

Something was wrong.

I stood there a while longer and then when I was done standing I reached into my pocket and took out the photograph of the target.

She was a girl. Young, maybe twenty, maybe not quite. She had black hair cut in a bob that was big at the back and small at the front and her bangs were so straight you could use them to survey a building. She had a small face made smaller by the thick, dark rings of eyeliner. She looked like an Egyptian princess.

This was Eva McLuckie. I wondered who she was. I wondered what she had done to get herself on someone's hit list.

As I stood on the spot I had a feeling I had known the answers to both of those questions yesterday.

I had just forgotten what those answers were.

And then Ada spoke.

"Ray, we need to talk."

I was all ears.

14

The Ritz-Beverly Hotel was a very particular kind of pile and one that was farther away than I thought. Farther still as I took the scenic route, weaving up and down and back and forth across West Hollywood—precautions seemed necessary, after what Ada had told me back at the office. It would have made the hairs go up on the back of my neck, if I had any. But thanks to Thornton, I still knew exactly what that felt like.

Eva McLuckie. She was our client—our *first* one, anyway. She was a movie star and she'd taken out a hit on another movie star, one Charles David. The only issue was that the current whereabouts of Mr. David were unknown, which meant I had to do a little of the old private detecting first just to find him. It seemed like a lot of work but as motivation went the amount of gold sitting in the brown athletic bag sitting by the desk in the outer office was right up there.

Then Ada told me about the Temple of the Magenta Dragon and the fact that our client Eva McLuckie had supposedly dropped out of the public eye herself—apparently in order to take out hits on her co-stars and host little meetings of her own particular kind of private club in the Temple's basement.

None of which made any particular kind of sense, but it was early days yet and I wasn't worried. So far, so good.

The real problem was what else had been lurking in the Temple basement. This problem made my circuits ache like a bad tooth.

This problem had a name.

Chip Rockwell.

I'd asked Ada to repeat everything to me twice, because the first time I wasn't sure I believed my audio receptors, even though I could have rewound and played it all back to myself. In fact, that's just what Ada did.

That wasn't all she played. She had my memory tape from the previous day lined up and she gave me the highlights. The dark basement and assembled crowd and the guy who Eva called "Mr. Rockwell" sitting there in his suit and bandages looking as much like a living human being as I did.

And that voice. I couldn't get it out of my circuits. It buzzed like a wasp, a monotone like a shorting wall socket had developed a voice and a bad temper.

Chip Rockwell. Movie producer, head of Playback Pictures. The big time. Even the soda jerk knew him.

I knew him, too.

Because I'd killed him.

Ada had told me about the job because I didn't remember it. Three years ago. Back when she called the shots while I slept on the job. The story went that Rockwell had fallen in with the mob and was using his studio to launder their money. Something must have gone wrong, because someone took out a contract with us on Rockwell's life, which I prematurely ended one dark and stormy night courtesy of a dangerous stairwell in the backlot of his own studio.

Chip Rockwell was dead. It had been big news.

But three years later the dead guy was sitting up in a basement

on Sunset Boulevard, in dinner jacket and bandages, talking
through some kind of machine.

Which meant he wasn't dead. Injured, and badly by the sound
of it, but not dead.

That was a problem. It meant that we hadn't fulfilled the contract.
If news of Rockwell's survival got back to the original client, chances
were they'd want their money back. Chances were they would want
far more than just money. And if Rockwell was still alive, he might
remember me and my late-night visit. Our little enterprise risked
exposure.

Except it had been three years. We hadn't had any trouble, according to Ada. Everyone thought Rockwell was dead. Still dead.
Which meant his current state of health was a secret. Which meant
we were still in the clear.

For now.

And then on top of this, the new job from the new client. One
that seemed to intersect the first in a way that neither Ada nor I
much liked.

I was to kill Eva McLuckie.

Now, this was hinky and we knew it. A little care was required
here. Sure, I could have found Eva and punched her ticket, but the
way the two jobs tangled was by no means coincidental. Couldn't
have been. Throw in Chip Rockwell and things weren't just tangled,
it was a *bona fide* Gordian knot.

So while Ada tried to go back to our new client for some more
information, I headed out to the Ritz-Beverly Hotel. Just for a look,
nothing more. If Eva was there, I wasn't going to kill her. She was
supposed to be calling the office for a daily update and I could give
it to her in person and then ask for an update of my own.

So I took the scenic route. I had a hunch that someone had seen
Eva come to the office yesterday, which meant she was being
watched. Then Ada reminded me of the mystery man on the road

above the Hollywood Sign and I had to concede the fact that maybe I was being watched, too.

At least I had been careful with the man from the Parks Department. Nobody had seen that.

Whether I had been paranoid or not didn't seem to make much of a difference, because for most of the way to the hotel I was in fact being followed by a gold coupe with a white roof that looked like you could pull it back if it was a nice day.

But it was a nice day now and the top was up. There was only one person in the car, and while he was making some kind of effort not to be seen, it wasn't working.

I figured I could deal with that problem when the time came and eventually I turned past the sign that said THE RITZ-BEVERLY HOTEL in a flowing script that looked like handwriting.

The hotel was a pink construction peeking out from behind rows of phoenix palms and another kind of palm with a narrow, tall trunk that I didn't remember the name of. The hotel was set well in grounds that were both capacious and sun-kissed. I reached the start of its driveway around ten in the morning and I was looking for lunch around the time I pulled into the guest parking lot. A sign told me valet parking was available at two bucks a day. I decided to do Ada a favor and use the free option so I parked the car in the shade of a palm to hide the paintwork. The building in front of me was pink and had curves and arches and three turrets that looked like Venetian bell towers. There were three flags fluttering against the blue sky, one per turret, the Stars and Stripes in the middle, flanked by the banner of the California Republic on either side. The windows, of which there were more than a few, had white frames and verandas with possibilities.

The place looked like an expensive kind of wedding cake, one that looked good in pictures but probably not so much up close.

I stood by the car in the shade of the palm tree and straightened my tie and my hat, trying to look like the kind of private detective who might be called to such an establishment by an exiled dowager duchess who had lost the family jewels in the top penthouse suite.

I walked toward the hotel and then I turned under the shade of the next palm tree along and watched the parking lot, but the gold coupe that had been following me all the way from Franklin didn't make an appearance. The tail—if he was a tail—wasn't *that* bad. But as I stood there a couple of cars cruised past the end of the driveway and kept on going. One of them could have been gold.

I was met at the hotel entrance by a phalanx of doormen in top hats and tails. Each of them smiled tightly and the oldest number opened a large gold-and-glass door for me. I doffed my hat and he did the same. I saw a red line around his forehead and his thin hair was damp.

Hell of a day to be wearing a getup like that.

The hotel lobby switched the pink for a yellowish cream. It was a better color in my book, except for the fact that it seemed to stick to everything like glossy pancake batter. The floor was yellowish cream marble. The marble pillars were the same. There were two desks about a mile away from me on either side. Between me and them was an obstacle course of sofas and easy chairs and side tables. The sofas and chairs were a yellowish cream and had enough padding to lose a small child in. The tables, made of a dark wood with an admirable grain, were mostly covered with yellowish cream tablecloths to hide their shame.

There was a piano in a sort of conservatory annex on my far left. The piano at least was black but the complexion of the man playing it matched the floor.

"May I help you, sir?"

An employee in a uniform that was too tight and a hat that was small and round appeared to my right. He had his hands clasped in front of him like a groom waiting at the altar for his bride, and when I looked at him he jerked his head up like he wanted to get that cap off real bad but regulations didn't allow him to touch it with his hands.

He smiled at me tightly so I returned the look. On the inside, anyway.

"I've got an appointment," I said. This was not strictly true.

"Yes, sir?" he said. What he really meant was "Yeah, me and my mother, too." He jerked his head back again. I was afraid he would give himself whiplash. "I'm sure reception can make a call to your party."

"Oh, that's okay," I said. "Private appointment. Fourth floor."

"Sir?"

"It's okay, I'm expected. McLuckie, room four-oh-seven. He's an army buddy."

The bellhop—I think he was a bellhop, hat like that, uniform with enough scrambled egg falling off the shoulder for the wearer to hold high rank in the army of a small tropical dictatorship—nodded but didn't offer any further argument, unless I was supposed to take some other meaning from the tight smile he turned on again.

I nodded at the elevators on the other side of the reception desks and he nodded back to me.

He didn't try to stop me as I walked over to the elevators and pressed the button. Before I stepped into the car I gave him a little wave.

He didn't wave back.

15

My destination was room 407 and the fourth floor seemed like a good bet. I cruised the corridor on carpet thick enough for a space capsule to make a splashdown on and spent some time appreciating the décor, which now featured some gilt in addition to the sickly cream. It looked like a lot of work and with good light from the big windows I had to admit it was pretty classy.

I glanced out said windows. I'd come around to the front of the hotel and I could see my car under my palm and all the other cars in the lot. Finally there was some life too, as a man and a woman with arms linked walked toward a convertible then unlinked arms as they went around opposite sides and got in. A moment later the engine turned over and they were chewing expensive white gravel all the way back to the street.

Then I turned back to the other cars in the lot, in particular my favorite gold coupe with the white roof, which had materialized in the sunshine opposite my car. Could have been a coincidence. It was a nice car. It was the kind of car that would be parked at a place like this, although I would have picked it to be one for valet, even at two bucks a day. The car was empty. I zoomed in to have a quick look. The angle I was at meant I couldn't see the driver's side too well but

I got a clean look at the passenger side. There was a newspaper sitting on red leather, both baking in the sun. I read half a headline about a movie premiere then zoomed back out and continued sliding silently down the corridor.

Soon enough the corridor windows disappeared as I headed deeper into the hotel and the chandeliers took over the job of lighting. They were nice, too. Crystal. Not too big. Elegant. I decided that I liked the way this hotel did things and I wondered what one of these elegant crystal chandeliers would look like in the office.

Four-oh-seven was, by my count, just around the corner. I kept on traveling.

Around the corner might have been 407 but the first thing I came to was a cleaning cart. It looked just as greasy and dirty as in any other hotel. There was a steel bucket and a mop and I counted four colored cloths hanging on a rail. Up top there were plastic squeeze bottles sitting in a tray.

Even though I was a machine, Professor Thornton had thought of everything, which meant my nose was pretty sharp. The whole ensemble in the corridor in front of me smelled like a swimming pool and the lady in the blue smock who came out of the open door of room 404 just next to the cart smelled like a can of furniture polish. It wasn't an unpleasant aroma.

She had black hair under a net and bags under her eyes, and her arms had a slackness in the upper portion that spoke of a certain age. As she backed out of the room she saw me and gave a little bow then turned her eyes to the floor.

"Sir," she said, then she waited. I was clearly supposed to be doing something. I watched her for a moment. He lips twitched like she wanted a cigarette, and she twisted an orange cloth in one hand like a rosary.

When I didn't move she looked up and then her eyes went wide.

Whether it was because I hadn't taken my hat off indoors or because underneath that hat was a face made of bronzed steel I wasn't sure. I put a bet on the latter. The orange cloth between her hands got so tight I thought it would make a pretty good garrote should she ever consider another line of work.

I lifted my hat to see if that helped and it did, because it made the cleaner smile. It was still a nervous smile but I was starting to get somewhere.

"Do you clean all the rooms on this floor?" I asked. It wasn't much of an introduction but I decided to skip formalities and get to business.

"Ah . . . yes, sir, I do," said the cleaner in a clear deep voice with a heavy accent. "Myself and Maria, sir, we clean four and three. I'm sorry, sir, but . . . do you need me to get you something?"

Her eyes narrowed. Her suspicions about robotkind had returned. I should have kept walking.

We were one step away from her placing a call to the front desk, saying there was a strange robot wandering around upstairs, so I reached inside my coat and pulled out my wallet. I opened it and showed it to her and held my hand there a while so she could get a good look. Her eyes crawled over the badge, reading every letter and every number.

Then her eyes moved up to my optics.

"*You're* a private detective?" she asked, like a guy made of metal couldn't hold down a good job.

"I am," I said in a low voice. I turned my shoulder and looked back down the empty passageway and then I bent down like I was letting her in on a secret. She seemed to get the drift, checking over her own shoulder before taking a step closer and ducking in for a conference.

"I'm looking for someone," I said.

The cleaner checked over her shoulder again. We were alone, swathed in cream woodwork with gilt edging and slowly sinking by the fathom into the carpet.

I pointed ahead with my shoulder. "Room four-oh-seven. You know who's in there?"

The cleaner stood tall and she bit her lip and looked back over her shoulder for the third time. She was considering something, but she wasn't sure of it.

I decided to get the jump on what she was thinking. I reached into my other pocket and pulled out my other wallet, the one I liked to keep paper money in. I opened it nice and wide and the cleaner got a good look at the contents. I picked out a one-dollar bill with two steel fingers.

"Room four-oh-seven," I said again.

"Four-oh-seven?" said the cleaner, still looking in my wallet. Her tongue appeared at the corner of her mouth and she lifted herself up onto her toes like a kid trying to see what secrets were at the bottom of the candy barrel. I lifted the dollar bill and folded it in one movement. I thought that was pretty smooth but she wasn't watching. Instead she pointed into my wallet. "Is that a two-dollar bill?"

My wallet was filled with ones and fives and tens. There might even have been a twenty or two at the back. But at the front, revealed by the buck I'd already pulled out, was a two-dollar bill. I hadn't noticed I was carrying it. Nobody liked the damn things, even though they were perfectly legal. I'd once heard of a guy who collected them and when he collected enough he stuck them all together and put them in a frame worth more than the money on display inside of it.

Maybe that guy was Thornton.

The cleaner's eyes were wide and glittering like a fortune-teller leaning over her crystal ball. So why not? I moved the wallet closer to her and she plucked the two-dollar bill with a finger and thumb, bringing it out slowly and carefully like the sides of my wallet were electrified.

Two bucks. I could have got the car valeted for that.

"Four-oh-seven?" I asked again, my eyes on hers and her eyes on her prize. She stretched the two-dollar bill and turned it this way and that to make sure it was real.

"Four-oh-seven is the honeymoon suite," she said.

"Oh," I said.

"But," she said, and then she dropped her hands and her eyes went narrow again and she dropped her volume to a whisper. Somehow that made her accent thicker and when she spoke I feared for the well-being of her tongue.

"But," she said, "I do not know what is going on in there." She checked over her shoulder, but there was nothing but thick carpet waving in the breeze like wheat in a field. "The room, it has been *ocupado* for, oh, I don't know. A long, long time. Maybe three months."

"Three months?"

"*Sí, sí.*"

I frowned, or at least it felt like I did. "That's some honeymoon."

The cleaner shrugged. I guess she had heard of stranger things in this town.

"So have you seen the happy couple?"

"*Sí*, but sir, I would not say they are happy."

"Oh?"

"No. They sound angry most of the time. But when they see us they stop talking."

I noted the information and I pumped for some more.

"Can you describe them?"

"Oh, well. She is small. Black hair. She wears too much makeup. Around the eyes." The cleaner mimed two rings around the eyes and I got the drift.

Eva McLuckie. One down.

"And the man?"

"Oh, oh."

"Tall? Short? Fat? Thin? Black? White?"

"Oh, I . . ."

"Beard? Mustache?"

"Beard! The man, he has a beard. A big beard. Very orange."

And there it was. Charles David.

The fact that Eva McLuckie and Charles David were apparently a couple was a surprise. I managed to hide it from the cleaner, which was pretty easy given I had no muscles in my face with which to change my expression.

"Have you seen them today?" I asked.

"Oh, oh, no, sir. Not for days. The woman, maybe . . . oh, Friday?"

"And the man?"

The cleaner shook her head. "Not for a long time. A week. Longer, I think. I can ask Maria?" Then her eyes did something that suggested she wanted some more of the money in my wallet.

"No, that's fine," I said. I nodded down the corridor. "Four-oh-seven?"

"*Sí, sí.*"

"Can you let me in?"

"*Sí, sí.*"

She led the way, her keys in one hand and the two-dollar bill in the other.

16

The inside of the honeymoon suite at the Ritz-Beverly Hotel was just as creamy as the rest of the place and the gilt that had started in the corridor came with me into the room. The main door led into a lounge not larger than a baseball field littered with gilt furniture. On my right was a hallway that ended in a big gilt archway with a big gilt set of double doors. The doors were closed. The whole place was spotless but when I turned to compliment the cleaner on her work she'd already gone and I stood there listening to her cleaning trolley swoosh down the hallway on the thick carpet. I was alone in the room with all that gold. It made me think of the athletic bag still sitting next to my desk back at the office.

The lounge was a dead end so I headed for the double doors. If a couple of newlyweds had been living here for three months then there would be plenty of evidence and my guess was that most of it would be beyond those doors in the master suite. There would be a closet full of clothes, drawers full of socks, a bathroom full of potions.

The fact that Charles David hadn't been seen for a week or more made sense. He'd fled. Maybe he knew his wife was after an early separation of a rather permanent kind. The fact that, according to the cleaner anyway, Eva herself hadn't been seen for a few days suggested to me that she'd bolted, too. She must have got wind of the price on her own head. Maybe that was why she hadn't called Ada yet.

Which didn't leave much for me to do in the honeymoon suite, but it was still worth a look. Maybe one of them had left clues about where they had gone. And there was always a chance they would be back, maybe if they'd left something important behind.

I got to the doors. A clock was ticking on the other side. It didn't sound like it was keeping particularly good time, like it needed winding or a new spring or both. I listened some more. Then I pushed the doors open once I was sure the room beyond was unoccupied.

The room I found myself in was wide enough to park four cars side by side on account of the fact it was empty, devoid not just of residents but of everything. The place had been stripped, leaving nothing but wallpaper and the thick cream carpet covered in a maze of indentations echoing where all the clutter that should have stood in the room had once been.

I'd heard—or maybe Thornton had heard—that fancy hotels could customize the furniture in your room at your request, but taking it all out seemed a step too far. If someone were here for three months they would have to sleep on something and the carpet was thick but not *that* thick.

The bedroom had three doors leading off of it, which seemed excessive.

The first door led to another bedroom that was smaller in the same way the White House was smaller than the Capitol. This room had also been cleared out, but where the bed should have been were instead two camp stretchers. They weren't wide enough for me to lie in but they looked comfortable enough for a person of regular dimensions. They were a deep green and the metal parts were painted a flat ocean gray. They were foldable. They were the kind of bed the army might use but not the kind of bed you expect to find in the honeymoon suite of one of your fancier Hollywood hotels.

The clock's ticking was louder in this room. I looked around but couldn't see any clock.

The second door led to a connected bathroom. I was shocked to discover it was done out in cream marble and gilt and what wasn't marble and gilt was mirrored. I looked at myself from four angles then checked the bath. It was dry. The basin too. Dry and clean. Immaculate. There were no hairs, nothing. If I hadn't known better I would have said the bathroom hadn't been used in about, oh, three months. I opened the cabinets and spent a couple of minutes counting folded towels and little bottles of hotel-branded shampoo.

Opening the third door that led from the master bedroom was like Christmas, given what I found on the other side.

This room had been emptied of the standard furniture, just like the others. In the middle of the room was a chair made of metal on a big metal revolving base. The chair consisted of three different parts to support the legs, body, and head, and had two long armrests. All of these parts were on an articulated frame, allowing the reclining patient to be lowered and raised, tipped and tilted. It was the kind of dentist's chair you could fly to Venus on.

Hanging above the chair was a big metal arm with several ball-and-socket joints allowing free movement in three dimensions. The arm was attached to the same base as the chair, and the part that hung over the chair ended in a four-pronged claw with sprung fingers, and a mirrored disk with a pointed cone in the center. This disk was on its own miniature arm, which sprang up from the wrist of the four-pronged claw and allowed the disk to be positioned independently in front of whatever it was that the claw was supposed to hold. The disk was no bigger than a bread plate and the pointed cone in the middle of it stuck out about two inches.

I didn't know what the contraption was for. I took a couple of pictures and listened to the ticking clock. There was no clock in this room, either.

And then I realized what it was. My Geiger counter was doing its best to get my attention. I frowned and told myself to do better. It was just that it had never gone off as far as I could remember (which today was about five hours) so I didn't expect to hear it.

I turned it up and I took some readings. It sounded like someone was grilling a steak in my head.

I headed back to the master bedroom, following the crackling. There was another door, next to the big set that led out. Somehow I'd missed it, but it didn't matter, because I didn't miss it now. As I got close the crackle got louder.

The door opened into a wide corridor, which after a couple of steps I realized wasn't a corridor. It was a walk-in closet, bigger (I guessed) than most of the regular hotel rooms. As I walked forward I slid open the sliding doors that lined either side of the passage. They were empty save for big chromed coat hangers permanently attached to the rails. Even in the honeymoon suite, the Ritz-Beverly didn't trust its guests all the way.

The passage ended in more sliding doors. I opened them. More space for clothes. Drawers here, big and wide and small and shallow. And underneath, at floor level, a big black rectangular safe.

My Geiger counter was now putting out a continuous howl. I feared for the safety of my new suit and hat.

The safe was locked. There was a combination dial on the front and a chromed handle. I turned the Geiger counter down and focused my audio receptors on the locking mechanism buried inside the safe's door. It didn't take long to crack the combination as I listened to the tumblers catch and engage and disengage.

Breaking into things was a useful skill in a job like mine.

Inside the safe was a box. I pulled it out. It was black plastic, and the plastic was textured, like it was pretending to be leather when it was anything but. The box was not quite a cube, a little taller than it was deep, ten inches high and eight square. The lid had a metal flip-catch, which I flipped.

The inner surface of the lid was lined with a metal that was dull gray and a little soft to the touch. Lead, but nowhere near enough of it to shield the outside world from the hot contents of the box. Under the lid was a stiff foam packer in two halves, the top half squeaking like a mouse in the jaws of a housecat as I pulled it out.

I looked into the box.

Inside was a square something. It looked like a cube made of frosted glass. Inside that glass was a tracery of filaments, like someone had printed a computer circuit on the inside of a giant ice cube.

I tilted the box this way and that to get a look. The sides of the box were also lead-lined. There was nothing else in the container. No label or writing or any kind, unless it was on the bottom, but I didn't much feel like taking a look. I figured I'd exposed the hotel to enough radiation today. So I put the top half of the foam spacer back in, closed the lid, put the box in the safe, closed it, and spun the dial.

Then I left the honeymoon suite as I had found it and headed for the hotel lobby.

There was a phone call I needed to make.

17

There was a different bellhop waiting for me in the lobby this time. His smile was nicer. There were two young ladies behind the reception desk on my left, one of whom was dealing with a hotel guest who was nothing more than two legs as thin as pins with a sphere of fur balanced on the top.

I pulled my collar up and my hat down and headed for the row of four wooden phone boxes that lay beyond the forest of soft furnishings, in an alcove that mirrored the spot where the piano was dropped. The pianist was still there, swaying on his stool with his eyes closed as he played. I didn't blame him. If I had to sit in the lobby for hours at a time I'd keep my eyes closed, too.

The booths had narrow double doors fitted with leaded stained glass. I went to the second booth along.

And then I turned to face the man sitting on the sofa opposite.

He had on a broad-brimmed fedora made of green rabbit felt, and he had his arms folded and his legs crossed tight. He looked uncomfortable and not at all concerned about the creases he was putting into his nice brown suit. His tie was red and it was pulled too tight as well, pinching the skin of his neck just below the waterline of a big orange beard. He wore dark glasses under the brim of his hat and he kept the brim down like I wouldn't notice him sitting there.

I stepped away from the telephones and closer to the man.

Charles David looked up at me but he kept everything folded tight. I couldn't see his eyes behind his glasses.

"It's the beard," I said. "Too distinctive. Stands out like a traffic light. Lose the beard. And maybe you'd make a better tail if you unwound and tried a bit harder."

He sighed and the sigh was a long one. He looked better in the photograph that was inside my jacket than in the flesh. I wasn't sure whether it was the fiery color of his beard that did it, but the skin of his face had a green tinge and there was a sweat on his brow. Altogether he looked a little seasick.

"That's what they said," he said, "but I told them, *no-can-do*. This beard is my livelihood. Do you know I have it insured for one million dollars?"

I whistled. It sounded like a truck making an emergency stop at the lights and made the bellhop and the two girls at reception and the ball of fur who was still arguing over a bill turn to look at me. I ignored them.

"Who's 'they'?" I asked, and then I started running through some options. I couldn't kill him here. I had to get him alone. Didn't matter much where. I had an entire hotel of rooms around me but after a second thought I discounted that idea. A movie star dies in the tub in his room and a lot of people would start talking about the big robot they saw in the lobby.

No, I had to get him somewhere else.

Charles David looked around. I followed his gaze. The others in the hotel lobby had gone back to their own business. Then he said, "Look, I don't have time for this," and then after a short pause he said, "We need to talk."

"Sure," I said. Sounded like getting him out of the hotel would be a little easier than I first thought. "Tell me," I said, "do you ever take down the top on that gold coupe, or do you worry about the upholstery getting faded?"

Before he could answer, the phone in the booth behind me rang. Charles David nearly jumped out of his skin but with his arms and legs all locked up he just jerked on the sofa and made it creak. His mouth formed an O with the million-dollar soup-catcher all around it.

"Excuse me," I said. "I think that's for me."

I went back to the second booth from the left. I couldn't fit into the box, so I reached in and picked up the receiver and stood there looking at the stained glass in the folded doors. In the scene, Sir Galahad seemed to be having some trouble averting his eyes from a woman in a thin white nightie with lace around the edges. They were standing in a forest. The woman was going to catch a chill, dressed like that.

On the telephone was nothing but a hazy white noise, like a waterfall in the distance.

"You'll never guess who I've run into," I said into the phone.

"I hope your trigger finger didn't get too itchy," said Ada inside my head. "You were supposed to just take a look, remember?"

"Don't worry. The girl isn't here. But I was tailed."

"By?"

"By a man with a beard worth one million dollars," I said. I wasn't sure whether I believed that or not but I thought Ada would get the picture.

"You're being tailed by Charles David?" asked Ada.

"I am," I said.

"Now there's a happy coincidence. Say, maybe he wants your autograph."

"No," I said, "what he wants is to talk."

"Talk?"

"Question is, do we want to listen?"

"What are you driving at, Ray?"

"This job. And the other one. They're fishy. I want to know what we're really getting ourselves into. Do you know what I found in room four-oh-seven?"

"I'm hoping you'll tell me."

"It's the honeymoon suite."

"Ooh, dishy."

"Not when the double king has been wheeled out and replaced by a nuclear-powered dentist's chair and the happy couple happens to be our pair of clients. They've been staying here three months, apparently."

The phone hissed in my ear. It sounded like rain on a hillside.

"Oh," said Ada. "Well, isn't that just tickety-boo?" Then there was a flicking sound, like someone trying to get a damp cigarette lighter to catch.

"I don't like it when you say tickety-boo, Ada."

"Do you think Eva McLuckie and Charles David are really married?"

"Not in the slightest. Whatever they are partners in, it isn't holy matrimony."

Ada paused and then she said, "Quite the three-pipe problem."

I didn't know what that meant so I ignored it. "Anything your end?"

"Not a peep. Can't get hold of our new client."

"And no call from McLuckie herself, right?"

"Got it in one," said Ada. "So what else was in the hotel room?"

I gave her the top-to-bottom description. After I'd sketched out the safe and the safe's contents, Ada made a humming sound.

"Okay," she said. "You left the box where it was?"

"I did. It's too hot to move. Lead-lined, but only just."

"You've probably soaked up a bit. You should come back to the office."

I checked my Geiger counter and it rattled off news I didn't much like but could have been worse. Ada was right. I wasn't quite a walking uranium rod but I didn't want to spread it around the rest of the hotel.

Ada asked, "Is Charles David still there?"

I glanced over. The movie star was still on the sofa. He was looking out the front windows of the hotel lobby.

"He is."

"Okay, Chief, listen up. He wants to talk to you, he can talk to you. Bring him back to the office with you."

"Isn't that a little risky?"

"He doesn't know what you do, Ray. He'll think you're a private dick, that's all."

"Eva McLuckie knows what I do."

"Well, depending on how the conversation goes, his visit to the office could be a once-in-a-lifetime trip, if you know what I mean."

I frowned on the inside as I watched Charles David just a few feet away. I pulled the telephone closer to my mouth.

Force of habit.

"Maybe he can tell us some more about what's going on at the Temple of the Magenta Dragon," I said. "I don't know if Rockwell lives in the basement or is just wheeled in for special occasions, but we still need to know where he's been for the last three years."

"You're right about that, Chief. So head back here. Give Charles the office address and he can drive himself. Probably best if you two aren't seen together."

I said okay and put the telephone back on the cradle. I motioned Charles David over.

"So you want to talk to me?"

Charles David nodded with quite some vigor.

"Fine," I said. "But not here." I gave him the address and I gave him Ada's instructions. Charles David nodded again, vigor intact, then left. It seemed a bit of risk, letting him out of my sight like that, but he seemed pretty interested in having a conversation and he seemed to like the idea that we could have it somewhere private like my office.

I waited a few minutes, then as I headed for the doors I thought about giving the pianist a two-buck tip only to realize he'd deserted his post. I wished him well in his escape.

The parking lot was where I'd left it, as was my car.

The gold coupe was gone.

18

I took the long way back to the office. It was just off the corner of Hollywood and Cahuenga Boulevards, but my detour was by way of La Brea Avenue, 8th Street, Hoover, then Western, and I had one optic on the traffic up ahead the whole way. There were plenty of coupes on the road and some were even gold but those that had removable lids were open and none looked to be driven by a man with dark glasses and facial hair insured for a sum big enough to fight a small land war over.

Just as intended. By my reckoning Charles David should have got to the office well ahead of me. He seemed to understand my request for discretion well enough.

But the traffic was heavy thanks to the lane closures around Grauman's Chinese Theatre and by the time I reached my building and went up to my office it was later than I would have liked.

He was hiding behind the door.

I could hear him breathing and I could see his shadow behind the frosted glass before I was halfway down the hallway outside the office. He was holding something I thought was probably a gun.

So much for a quiet chat. Still, that was okay. Guns didn't worry me.

The door was unlocked. He must have had a skeleton key. I didn't loiter. I opened the door and I walked in and then I stopped in the middle of the outer office. The door to the computer room was closed. From beyond the door came the sound of someone typing, which I knew was really micro-switches flipping.

There was another sound. A click. I was right about the gun.

I turned around.

Charles David had the coat and the hat and dark glasses on and that famous beard was glistening with droplets of sweat like someone had thrown a handful of diamonds onto a grass lawn. He looked hot and bothered and in need of a Pepto-Bismol. His gun was pretty interesting. A pistol, automatic. Pretty big, too. A Beretta maybe. It looked new and it was probably expensive for anyone who wasn't a big-time movie star.

I glanced over at the computer room door. I wasn't afraid for myself and my radioactive suit was on the way out anyway. But I was a little worried about Ada. A man with a gun and an idea could do a lot of damage if he got in there.

Then again, nobody knew about her, and if Charles had read the stencil on the door he'd just have thought I was a private detective.

One he wanted to talk to at the point of a gun, apparently. He didn't say anything as he pointed it at me, but he did sway on his feet a little.

I frowned, somewhere. "You feeling okay, bub?"

Bub smiled and showed me a lot of white Hollywood teeth. My frown lit up the circuits down one side of me and back up the other like a jukebox.

There was a streak of blood across his two front teeth.

"Oh yeah, oh yeah," said Charles, and he waved the gun up and down like he preferred to nod with that rather than his head. Maybe he didn't want to mess that famous beard up any.

The phone on the desk rang. I knew who it was. I didn't move.

Charles didn't either but his eyes moved to it and his mouth opened again like it had back at the hotel. He seemed to find telephones worrisome.

Then he nodded with the gun again. "This happen to you a lot?"

If I had an eyebrow to raise I would have. "People don't use the telephone to talk to you?"

Charles didn't seem to like this. His eyes went around the room then came back to my face. "Someone's watching you, aren't they? They called at the hotel and now they're calling here." He ground his molars. I could tell by the way the beard moved at the back of his jaw. "They're everywhere," he said in a low voice. "They get everywhere, get to everyone, everyone."

I had a feeling he was talking mostly to himself.

The telephone jangled.

"Or," I said, "I'm just a popular robot. Do you mind?"

Charles dragged a hand across his damp forehead but his hand was as sweaty as his face so all he did was move moisture around. Then he nodded with the gun, which I took to be a yes.

I walked to the desk and picked up the phone. "Raymond," I said into the speaking end.

The phone hissed uselessly in my left audio receptor and Ada exhaled a nonexistent lungful of smoke in my mind.

"You found out what two-first-names wants yet?"

I lifted the telephone from the desk so as not to stretch the cable any and looked Charles up and down.

"Not quite," I said and at that Charles perked up, lifting his chin and standing on his toes like a ballerina getting her cue.

"How does he look?" Ada asked.

"Like he's eaten a plate of bad oysters. He's sick, isn't he? And you know he's sick."

Two-first-names didn't seem to be bothered about being talked about in the third person.

"It was just a hunch," said Ada. "So start talking to him. I'll wait here."

I nodded and put the phone down.

"You *are* a popular robot," said Charles. He was smiling again and had returned his heels to the floorboards. "You should be in pictures." There was still blood on his teeth.

I laughed. It sounded like a garbage truck grinding its gears in a low tunnel. "Y'know," I said, "I don't think you're the first person to say that."

"So you're a detective?" asked Charles.

I looked at the gun in his hand. It looked heavy. I looked at his face.

"Yes. Private investigator, licensed by the city. Do you normally wave handguns at licensed private investigators?"

Charles tilted the gun like he had to read the engraved model number on the side. His eyes were invisible behind the opaque glasses. With his mouth open he looked surprised. He swayed on his feet again.

"Ah . . ." he said, and then he said, "Ah," again.

Then he pointed the gun back at me. "They gave it to me."

"Who's they?"

"What were you looking for at the hotel?"

"I was looking for a woman. Still am. I was led to believe she had a room at the Ritz-Beverly Hotel, but she wasn't there."

"I . . . what?" asked Charles. His beard moved in a way that seemed to indicate a state of confusion.

I reached into an inside pocket and pulled out the photograph. I straightened it out and I held it the right way around for him to look at.

Charles pointed at the photograph with his gun. "That's Eva Mc-Luckie."

I tossed the photograph onto the desk. "I know," I said.

Charles coughed. It was dry. When he was done he heaved a breath and I saw more blood on his teeth.

He was sick. Ada knew it and now I could see it for myself.

I wondered how much radiation a normal man, even one with a big, full beard, could take before he got ill.

Before he got dead.

Charles coughed again and pinched his nose with his free hand like his sinuses were about to blow.

"You are working together on something?" I asked.

"Ah, yes, you could say that. I mean, we *were*. Before everything." He waved the gun around to indicate the entirety of the world around him.

"Before everything what?"

"Before they found out. They're all in on it. Eva, too. I knew she wouldn't last long, but I had hoped it would be longer—*argh!*"

He let the gun droop in his grip as he took his free hand from his nose and plunged it into his jacket. He fumbled then pulled out a small plastic cylinder. He popped the lid with his thumb, all the while trying to keep the gun pointed somewhere in my general direction.

His thumb slipped and the container dropped. Small white pills hit the rug and scattered like a teenage gang caught drinking in the street.

"Ah, dammit," said Charles. He bent awkwardly at the knees while trying to keep his upper body straight and trying to reach the pills. I moved forward to help but he jerked back and nearly fell over. His glasses slipped to the end of his nose and the eyes behind those glasses were red raw. Then he brought the gun up high. "Stop right there," he said. He stepped forward, treading on some of the pills. He seemed to have forgotten about them.

"You don't look good, Mr. David," I said.

At this Charles laughed. "Don't I know it," he said. "There's no way out of this one for me. I should have known, of course. First Fresco and Alaska. Then Eva. They've got them all. All that work, gone, gone. But I had to try, didn't I?"

I looked Charles David in his bloodshot eyes.

"Who's got them? Where's Eva now, Charles? What were you try-ing to do?"

Charles laughed. He adjusted his grip on the gun and he adjusted the glasses on his nose.

"Charles! You wanted to talk, so let's talk. What were you trying to do?"

"Enough!"

"Talk to me, Charles. What's going on?"

He laughed again. "What's going on is this, Detective."

Then he pulled the trigger.

19

Like I said, guns don't worry me. I have a bronze steel chassis reinforced with titanium and some alloys that Professor Thornton invented and the federal government was pretty pleased with.

But while guns don't worry me I was sure someone else in the building or the street outside would hear the shots and call the police and that I could do without.

But nobody called the cops because nobody heard the gun. Nobody heard the gun because it didn't fire.

Charles didn't seem to notice. He held it up and pulled the trigger and it went *click-click-click-click*.

"You've got the safety on," I said.

Charles made a surprised expression and he turned the gun again to look at the side of it. He swore, fussed with a switch, then turned the gun back on me. But while he'd been fussing I'd moved closer and before he tried the trigger again I placed a big hand over the muzzle and pulled slightly. The gun slid out of his sweaty grip with the greatest of ease. His arm hung there in the air for a second or two. Then he let it swing by his side.

"Charles," I said, "what's going on? Did somebody put you up to this?"

Charles didn't answer. Instead he grabbed his chest and moaned, and stumbled forward. I let him go. He hit the edge of the desk and leaned over it, gasping for air.

He was sick all right.

I went over and grabbed his shoulders and turned him around. He went with the motion, flopping like a dead fish. His dark glasses were pointed at me. I pulled them off and tossed them on the desk. He screwed his eyes closed and winced in pain, like the light in the office was just too bright.

"Charles, come on," I said. I lifted the gun up, holding it by the barrel. Maybe that would jog his memory. "Is this thing yours or did somebody give it to you?"

He opened an eye. He looked at the gun. He nodded. "It was issued to me."

"That a fact?"

"It is."

"Issued by whom?"

Charles coughed. I let him go. He turned back around to lean on the desk. "The CIA."

I frowned on the inside. "What, the CIA goes handing out firing pieces to movie stars, now?"

Charles laughed, and then the laugh turned into a cough that ended with a wet sort of slurping sound. He ran a hand over the back of his mouth. It came away bloody.

"I'm with them," he said, wheezing. "They recruited me, about a year ago. I'm an agent. Undercover. *Deep* undercover. They had me investigating un-American activities in the motion picture business."

Un-American activities?

Perhaps like, oh, a certain bunch of Russians meeting in the basement of a Hollywood nightclub? But since when did the CIA operate on American soil? Wasn't that beyond their jurisdiction?

I was about to ask Charles about the very same but before I could he nodded at the photograph in front of his nose.

"Who sent you to find her?" he asked.

"The thing about being a private detective," I said, "is that it's *private*. That information is between me and my client, who shall remain nameless." I left out the fact that I had no idea who the client was, along with the fact that I wasn't sent to find her but to kill her.

Charles hissed in pain or anger.

"You don't get it, do you, tin man?" he said. "I was sent in to uncover a Communist plot against this great nation, and that's exactly what I've found!"

A Communist plot. A movie star—Charles—sent deep undercover by the CIA?

Oh, I was starting to get it, all right.

"Listen," I said. "I believe you. I saw your co-star Eva McLuckie and her Red pals having a little dinner meeting just last night. Do you know what they're planning?"

Charles heaved a breath. "It's big. Very big." Then he coughed and there was a pattering sound, like a cat pawing at a mouse trapped behind an air vent. It kept going and going and then I looked down at the desk and saw red splashes on Eva McLuckie's face. Then I looked up and saw Charles was looking down at the picture, too, and he had his free hand to his face. That expensive beard was now stained a brilliant scarlet and more of the red stuff was coming out of his nose.

The telephone started to ring. I ignored it.

"You're not well," I said. "It's radiation poisoning, isn't it, Charles?"

Charles didn't like that statement. Not one bit. He yelled something that didn't have much in the way of words and he swooshed his arms over the desk, sending Eva McLuckie's face spinning over the edge. Then he grabbed the telephone and yanked it. He yanked it so hard that he pulled the cable clean out of the socket, and then he fell backward and into the chair in front of the desk that used to be reserved for clients.

"I'm doing this for my country, dammit!" he yelled. "And you're part of it. You're part of it!"

"Part of what? Tell me, Charles. Tell me and maybe I can help."

Charles laughed and coughed up more blood and laughed again. Blood flew from his mouth and hit the rug.

"Help? My God, help? You're the problem. I came here to take you out, you stupid tin can. It's the only way left to stop it. Don't you see? You, too. You're part of it, too!"

His gun was still in my hand. I squeezed it a little.

"It takes more than a peashooter to scratch my chassis, son," I said. "And like it or not, I'm as red as President Kennedy."

Charles shook his head. Then he coughed and when he spoke he had to punctuate his words with big gulps of air. "I had it all ready. All set up. But she was one of them. One of them. She couldn't resist, not for so long. Me, neither. It was too much. And now. Now. Nothing left. But if I could take you out. Then they couldn't finish. Couldn't finish. Couldn't finish. Phase four couldn't finish."

I had a feeling my time with Charles David was running out.

"What's phase four?" I asked. "Charles, listen to me. I know about the Soviet cell. Tell me about Rockwell. Chip Rockwell. He's running it, right? Do you know what happened to him?"

Charles's eyes opened like doves taking flight. "Yes," he said. "Rockwell, Rockwell . . ."

"What about Rockwell? Where is he now? What is he doing?"

Charles coughed. More blood came. A cupful, at least. It poured out of his mouth and down his beard and onto his shirt.

"We can help you, Charles," I said. "And you can trust me. You're sick, but I can get you patched up. But you have to listen to me, Charles. What's their plan? What's phase four?"

Charles blinked like he'd just woken up. He reached out and

curled his fingers, his eyes wide. I figured he had something to say and not long to say it. I turned my audio receptors up.

"Phase four," said Charles David. "They're almost ready for phase four." His voice was a croaky whisper.

"Yes, phase four," I said. "What is it? Charles, stay with me. Do you know what phase four is?"

"You are, tin man," he said. "You are."

"What?"

"You are phase four," whispered Charles David, "but maybe there's time. Phase three. Stop phase three and you stop phase four."

I frowned on the inside. I was losing him.

"What's phase three, Charles?"

"Friday," he said. "Friday." Then he shook his head. "The house. You'll find it in the house. You'll need it. I had it all ready. All ready."

I was going to ask him what was all ready but then Charles David grabbed the arms of the chair and pushed himself to his feet. I took a step forward and reached for him but he leaned on the desk again and waved me away. He stood like that with his head down, taking deep breaths. Seemed like he was recovering a little.

"Charles? What's at the house? What's on Friday?"

He shook his head again.

Then he yelled and launched himself at me. I was surprised and whether by accident or design, Charles took advantage of that fact. I was heavy and didn't move but he wasn't trying to fight me.

Instead he went for the gun still in my hand. Charles grabbed it and pulled, and I pulled back, dragging him toward me. He hit my chassis with his and he looked up into my optics and he kept pulling at the gun.

That's when there was a loud bang and Charles David's body jerked, once. He was still looking at me when I released my grip and let his body fall. His head clipped the side of the desk as he went down but I don't think he felt a thing. As he lay on the office floor on his stomach, a pool of blood began to grow underneath him, not from his nose and mouth this time but from a hole somewhere in his gut. The gun was still in his hand, finger still on the trigger.

I frowned on the inside, then went over to the computer room door and opened it. Ada's tapes spun and her lights flashed but she didn't speak.

"Charles David is dead," I said.

"So I heard. I guess we can keep the gold, then."

"It was an accident. He went for the gun."

"I believe you."

I looked back at the body on the floor. "He was sick. Radiation poisoning, right?"

"He was exposed," said Ada. "More than the others, though. That's interesting."

I walked over to the late movie star. On the floor around him and the blood were the white pills from his bottle and everything he'd pushed off from the desk. That included his glasses.

I picked them up. They were big and heavy, the lenses thick and tinted a deep gray-green. They were plastic, not glass. They looked less like sunglasses and more like the kind of eye protection you needed when welding.

Or working with something else dangerous.

Something . . . *radioactive,* perhaps.

I mulled over the actor's final lines. I felt that shiver again and I turned back to the computer room and eyeballed a spot somewhere near the ceiling.

"So whatever is going down," I said, "it's going down on Friday."

"Seems so."

"You know what else is going down on Friday?"

"Do tell."

"The nationwide premiere of that movie, *Red Lucky.*"

"Oh, I don't like that connection, Ray."

"Neither do I," I said. "And then there's the house. I'll find what I need at the house. Whose house? *His* house?"

"Could be, Ray."

"Get me the address. I need to go take a look."

"Coming right up, Chief. But do you want to clean up the mess first?"

Charles David lay cooling on the bloodstained rug. I checked my Geiger counter. The reading was a little warm but nothing I felt worried about.

"Someone would have heard the gunshot and called it in," I said. "The cops will be on their way. Maybe we need to leave this one to the proper channels."

"Let me handle the proper channels," said Ada. "For the moment I suggest we keep the sudden demise of famous film star Charles David our little secret for now."

"Because?"

"Because we want to keep tabs on Eva McLuckie. She's supposed to be calling for updates."

"But she hasn't yet."

"No," said Ada, "but she might still. The longer we can keep her on a lead, the more time we have to follow that lead back to Rockwell."

"I got it," I said, and then I took off my hat and I got to work.

20

When I woke up it was Thursday and I had work to do. Charles David's house was the kind of Spanish Colonial Revival that *Better Homes and Gardens* would pitch a fit over. It was perched on a slope on a street that was perched high in the Hollywood Hills. The street was narrow and mine was the only car on it. The residence had a big, black iron gate right on the street, framed by tall stucco walls capped in terra cotta that formed the outer perimeter of the movie star's private domain. Beyond the gate I could see a driveway that was long and curved around a lawn about the size of a football field.

I passed the gate and found a spot to pull up in and walked back down the street. It was a little steep. I stood by the gates and admired their craftwork. They had bars twisted into the shapes of tree branches and there were black iron birds sitting on those branches. At the top and bottom, framing the whole thing, were stylized beehives, complete with orbiting bees.

From here I could see the driveway ended in a capacious three-door garage that sat underneath one wing of the movie star's mansion. The garage doors were closed.

The gate was secured by a chain and a padlock. I unsecured it and stepped through, sticking to the edge of the great lawn and the limited cover provided by a row of palm trees that skirted the edge. The big house towered over the lawn on two sides. On the third a retaining wall and hillside above marked the boundaries of the property.

I stopped behind the second palm. There was movement ahead. One of the garage doors opened. There was no car inside but a man with suntanned skin appeared. He was dressed in green coveralls and carrying a rake. He shuffled around and grabbed something I couldn't see. Then he exited the garage pushing a wheelbarrow and made a tight right turn. There was a gate painted green at the side of the house. He opened it and went through. The gate banged shut of its own accord.

I waited a moment to be sure the gardener had gone. I listened to the birds and the bees. It was a beautiful warm afternoon and that great big green lawn with stripes in it glittered with dew like a starscape in front of me.

Of course, a star like Charles David had to be surrounded by people, and not just gardeners. He had to have staff. A maid at least, maybe more than one. Cooks and cleaners. Secretaries and personal assistants. A manager and an agent. Chances were some of them were inside the house right now and none of them yet knew their star employer's light had been snuffed clean out.

With the coast clear and no other movement around the house or in any of the multitude of windows that overlooked the lawn and driveway, I headed up to the house on the grass. Then I stopped and I headed up the driveway proper when I realized I was leaving a trail in the wet lawn.

The front door was a big double event made of dark wood with metal bands across it like it had come from a castle. I decided to leave it unmolested and went for the obvious option. The garage. The third door was still up and beyond the door there would be an internal door leading into the mansion itself.

The three-car garage was two-thirds full with a red Ferrari and a silver something that shared the same low angles of the Italian number and looked just as expensive. I was standing in the empty space that I guessed was home to a gold coupe with a white top. A more sensible car, the kind of car you cruise around town in, tailing people if the urge comes to you.

There was a door at the side behind the red automobile and there were stairs behind the door.

I went up.

Inside I came out into an atrium big enough to hold a three-ring circus with plenty of airspace for the flying trapeze.

I waited there a moment, turning up my audio receptors. I could hear the gardener outside, around the back, and I could hear the birds tweeting and the buzz of bees from the same direction. The bees in particular were loud. That explained the hive motif on the main gates. Of course Charles David kept bees. That much money, I'd keep bees, too. Why wouldn't you?

I could hear just two people in the house, both on this level. One male, one female, their voices echoing in such a way that suggested they were sitting in a tiled kitchen not larger than the Hollywood Bowl. Two of David's staffers, as expected.

What I hadn't expected was the language they were talking in. Because it sure wasn't English. The accent was a real mouthful, the words complex with plenty of rolling consonants.

Russian. I'd put two whole dollars on it.

I struck off the kitchen from my list of rooms to search. That was fine by me. Charles David had been nonspecific about what I was going to find in the house, but if you want to learn about someone and their secrets, you head for the bedroom. You'll find all you need in there.

There was a broad set of stairs curving around the wall of the entrance hall so I took them up two full turns of the screw before I found myself on a thickly carpeted landing with too many doors. None of them were what I wanted. A house this size, the master bedroom would be about as far away from the front door as possible. Charles David would want to keep an eye on his bees, after all.

The master bedroom was at the back. The door was closed and locked, so I picked the lock and stepped in and then closed the door behind me. I took one step farther and took the scene in.

It was a mess. It was also dark, one wall of blackout drapes pulled tight. I didn't need the light, I just turned my optics up.

The room had enough square footage to sell used cars in and most of the floor was covered with the biggest Oriental rug I had ever seen, which considering I couldn't remember before six that morning maybe wasn't saying so much. The bed was against the far wall and was circular, which just seemed confusing. It had on it a scattering of pillows and some blankets and sheets that were patterned. The bedding was tangled up, the bottom sheets pulled away to show the mattress beneath.

The floor between me and the bed was covered in clothes and shoes. No wonder Charles David kept the room locked. The maids would have a fit if they saw it. But I didn't think that was all he was hiding.

Firstly, the room stank. Not just because it was closed up and warm and musty and the sheets and clothes were dirty. There was something else. The smell of a hospital, not the sharp tang of disinfectant but what lay underneath.

The scent of sickness, of blood.

Secondly, the room was *hot*. My Geiger counter kicked into gear as soon as I stepped through the doors, then settled into a constant but angry rattle.

Charles David was keeping his illness a secret from his staff. He was also trying to keep his staff safe from what I really hoped I wasn't about to find.

I walked the half-mile to the bed and saw it. The sheets were Egyptian cotton with a thread count I'd need Ada to calculate. But they were not patterned. They were covered in blood. The pillows, too. Beside the bed was a pile of towels, monogrammed in gold with the initials CDW. They were dry but as stained as the sheets with blood. CDW's, I supposed. I wondered what the W stood for. Seemed like everyone in this town had a fake name.

There was a bathroom connected to the bedroom, about an acre of black and white tile and what at first I thought was a swimming pool before I realized it was a bath. It was empty but dirty, a dark ring around the circumference and something that glistened a dark brown around the plug hole. There was more of it congealed on the floor in splashes.

I checked the cabinets. They were stuffed with junk. Headache pills. Half-done aftershaves fermenting like corked wine and blunt safety razors that left brown rust stains on the white shelves. I wondered what Charles David looked like without his beard and how long it had been since his chin had seen that famous Hollywood sunshine.

I went back to the bedroom. I opened the closet. Charles David had an expensive collection of suits and shoes. This I expected. He also had a whole section dedicated to ties and handkerchiefs, all arranged on racks like a magazine stand.

What I didn't expect but what I wasn't surprised to see were the black smocks and the rubber gloves. The smocks were hanging in the closet and were wrapped in plastic like they'd just come from the cleaners, and the gloves were wrapped in the same and sat on the shelf underneath. I picked up a pair of gloves and saw their plastic wrap was sealed. They were new and unopened.

I left them where they were and turned back to the bed. One advantage of the room being such a mess was that nobody would notice if I turned it over myself, so I did.

Nothing. Dirty clothes, bloodstained towels. Our movie star had been having some rough nights.

The bedside cabinet was more bountiful. There was just one, against the wall. It had a cupboard and a drawer. I opened both.

In the drawer was a notebook. It was filled with numbers written in red ink, in groups of four digits. The notebook didn't have "CIA" printed on the front but I knew enough to see it was a codebook of some kind.

In the cupboard underneath the drawer were arranged five bottles. Two big, three small, each with a different label, each filled with pills and tablets in five different sizes and colors.

The labels on four of the bottles weren't standard. They were white paper and there was no name or address of the patient, no drug company branding or instructions to take two with water and avoid swimming or driving forklift trucks. Instead, on each label there was just a string of letters and numbers, and underneath that another, larger number. The numbers were in sequence, one through four.

Whatever they were, they weren't prescription drugs.

The label on the smallest bottle had plenty to say. I lifted it up to take a closer look.

"Well, that's unsettling," I said to nobody.

The label said POTASSIUM IODIDE and underneath that was a big, yellow, circular sticker. The sticker had a central black dot and three arcs of black floating off the middle like the blades of a propeller.

It was the symbol for nuclear energy. But that bottle wasn't hot. Potassium was radioactive itself but only slightly. According to my Geiger counter the bottle was about as hot as a bunch of bananas, which is to say not very.

What my Geiger *was* telling me, as I crouched by the cabinet, was that there was a monster under the bed.

I scooped up all five bottles and spaced them out around the pockets of my jacket and trench coat. Maybe Ada would know what the pills were for and what the codes meant.

Then I ducked down to look under the bed. As I put one hand on the mattress I discovered the circular bed was on a turntable that moved under my weight.

Movie stars, huh?

The turntable had a pedestal base but was designed so you could still stow stuff out of sight under the bed. There was something stowed. I reached in and pulled it out.

It was a valise, all hand-tooled leather with fine gold stitching, the kind of bag where the label on the inside would be written entirely in Italian and if you had to ask how much it cost that meant you couldn't afford it.

There was something soft in the bag. I unzipped it and my Geiger counter went into overdrive. I stood up and held the bag with one hand and yanked out a bundle of clothing with the other. It was a black fabric, thin and artificial, something like a shower curtain or the cape a barber might hide a customer under.

Something like the plastic-sealed smocks that were hanging in Charles David's closet behind me.

I began to unravel the parcel. Something small but heavy tumbled onto the circular bed, making a sound as it hit the gathered blankets like a large cat jumping into a basket of fresh laundry.

I reached down and pulled a frosted glass cube from the tangle. It was four inches on each side but was heavy, like it wasn't made of glass but of something else, like stone or natural crystal.

I held it up to a useful sliver of light coming in through the gap in the blackout blinds. The cube had something in it, a crisscrossing of filaments that looked like printed circuitry.

It was the same as the cube I'd left back at the Ritz-Beverly Hotel.

Like that cube, this number was radioactive. Not enough to cook a person from the inside out, but enough to make a man very sick if, say, he slept twelve inches above it every night.

I wrapped the cube back up in the smock and stuffed the package back into the bag. Then I paused and unloaded the pill bottles from my pockets into it. Everything was pretty snug and nothing would get broken, and I figured Charles David wasn't going to be asking for his secret stash anytime soon so I might as well take the whole lot back to the office.

I left the bedroom and closed and locked the door after me. I went back down the hallway and paused at the top of the stairs. Someone was still in the kitchen. There was a crinkle and crackle and this time it wasn't from my Geiger counter. They were reading a newspaper or a magazine. From the garden out the back drifted another conversation between a man and a woman. A conversation being conducted in Russian.

I could have searched the rest of the house, but the longer I lingered, the more chance I'd be caught. And I figured I'd found just what Charles David had been talking about.

I let myself out through the garage.

21

When I got to the car, I pulled away, drove up the street a little, then turned around and found a spot closer to the David mansion. I sat in the car watching the house through the gates while I wired Ada a couple of the pictures I'd taken inside. A quarter-hour later the telephone rang in the cradle beside me.

I watched the gardener reappear through the side gate as I picked up the receiver. The gardener went inside the garage, then came out and unzipped his coveralls, then peeled the top half off and tied the arms around his waist before getting down to work at the flowerbed right bang next to the front doors. I'd left right on time.

I told Ada this and she laughed inside my head.

"You're in a better mood," I said.

"You gotta laugh at something, Chief."

The gardener was getting a sweat up as the sun got higher and hotter. I zoomed in a little. He was built pretty well and his skin was slick with the results of his labors.

Underneath that perspiration was something else. Tattoos. Lots of them. An eagle and some other stuff, along with some writing. None of it in English. Cyrillic. I couldn't read any of it and the symbols didn't mean anything to me, but I checked how much film I had left in my chest and took a couple of souvenirs.

It sounded like Ada was pulling on a cigarette, but I knew that was my imagination. I ignored the image and told her about the contents of Charles David's bedroom.

"Do you know what they use potassium iodide for?" she asked, blowing a lungful of imaginary smoke over my head. There was a creak like she was leaning back in the chair behind my desk again, feet up on the blotter.

The front door of the mansion opened and a woman came out. She looked like a maid and she was carrying a tray with a tall, fat jug and two glasses. I didn't know what was in the jug but the gardener was sure as hell pleased to see her.

"Let me guess," I said. "Radiation poisoning. Right?"

"Aw, Ray!" She laughed again, the laugh as tall and fat and cool as the contents of the jug that the maid was now pouring for the gardener. "What gave it away?"

"Just a little yellow warning sign on the outside." I watched the gardener and the maid share a joke. "Didn't help him much, did it?"

"Nope," said Ada. "Charles 'Two First Names' David was a hot ticket, and not just at the box office. A ticket that was well and truly punched."

The maid and the gardener sucked the last of their drinks and then they sank to the grass and started sucking on each other's faces. I left them to it and glanced down at the valise on the passenger seat.

"So the potassium was no good?"

"It should have worked," said Ada, "up to a point, anyway. Maybe he stopped taking the pills. Or maybe having that thing underneath him every night was just too much."

"Maybe he didn't know."

"He knew enough to have a bottle of potassium iodide in the nightstand."

"And the other bottles?"

"No idea."

"What about the pills he spilled on our rug?"

"Well," said Ada, "I could whip up a chemical analysis, but that would take a while. But we can compare them with the others when you get back."

I asked about the strange labels. Ada smoked thoughtfully for a few seconds. I mentioned the codebook I'd left in the bedside cabinet.

"If TFN was a secret agent, I'd assume his masters gave him the potassium. They must have given him the other bottles, too."

I frowned on the inside. "TFN?"

"Two-first-names."

"Oh," I said. "So those other bottles were other anti-radiation drugs?"

"Could be. Experimental maybe, given the coded labels."

"Well, they didn't do him much good either."

It felt like Ada shrugged. The sensation made my circuits tingle across the ridge of my back.

"I did say *experimental,* Ray."

"Okay," I said, and I adjusted the car phone's receiver and began untangling the coiled lead with my fingers. "So Charles David was badly affected while his famous buddies seem to be okay. They were all wearing that special gear at the club. Charles, too. He has a closet full of the stuff. But it wasn't enough."

"Right," said Ada. "They were all exposed. Your friend Fresco had a box of pills at the club himself, if you remember."

"You know I don't. But I'm willing to bet they might be the same as what's in one of Charles's bottles. Only they didn't work for Charles because he got closer than the others. Close enough to get sick." I looked back at the valise. "Close enough to acquire a souvenir."

"Because he was snooping for the CIA."

I watched the house and the two people twisting in front of it.

"He said he was deep undercover," I said. "I think I believe him. His personal staff all seem to be Russians."

"Russians?"

"I'm wiring some more pictures."

"You're a doll, Chief."

I considered the bag I'd borrowed again. Inside was the radioactive glass cube. Same as the one at the hotel. Charles David had a closetful of protective gear, and at the secret meeting in the basement of the Temple of the Magenta Dragon everyone wore the same. Because there was something in that basement that was radioactive, too.

I had a feeling I knew exactly what it was.

Chip Rockwell.

I told Ada the same and she made a whistling sound. "From movie producer to nuclear man?"

"Well," I said, "he wasn't much of a man. Just a suit and a voice."

"And a radioactive cube?"

I shrugged in the car seat. "There could have been anything under those bandages."

I looked up and out across that big lawn. I could see nothing but one of the maid's feet, raised in the air, her shoe swinging off her big toe. Seemed like a nice day for some yard work and I supposed even foreign spies were allowed some downtime.

Ada made a sound that was like the stirring of a mug of coffee that only existed within the matrix of her master program.

"Has Eva called?" I asked.

"Not a word."

No surprise there. "Have you reached the client who took out the contract on her yet?"

"No dice," said Ada. "Feels like they went to a lot of trouble to keep themselves hidden."

"Okay. I need to get into that basement at the club."

"You think Rockwell is still there?"

I frowned on the inside. "He's the key to all this and it's time I paid a visit. If he's both radioactive and trying to stay dead then a deep basement seems like a good place to hide." I shifted in my seat. In an effort to avert my gaze from what was going on up on that great big green lawn I turned to look out the back window.

"Okay, Ray," said Ada, "but be careful—"

"Hold that thought."

"What is it?"

"I've got company."

A black car had pulled up just down at the bend. There was a man in the car wearing a wide-brimmed hat. The car was still running.

I zoomed in as much as I could, but then the man changed gears and pulled the car out and around mine. He floored it and sped up the slope, the car bucking on the rear axle like a lion taking down a gazelle.

"I heard that, Ray. Who was it? Another tail?"

"Could be Charles David's handler, perhaps. If he was a CIA asset they'll have someone keeping an eye out."

"A someone who will start wondering where that asset is," said Ada.

"Or it could be more Russian agents," I said. "Ada, I'll call you back," and before she could say another word I dumped the dead telephone back on the cradle that sat between me and the passenger seat.

The black car was ahead of me at the end of the street, but was still in sight. Just.

I turned the ignition and pressed my foot to the floor.

22

The man in black was good, I gave him that. Better than Charles David, anyway. The black car he was in was a pig, the suspension soft as anything, the thing pitching and yawing like a small plane about to make an unscheduled touchdown.

But he was a good driver doing his best work and he knew what he was doing. He took me out of the Hollywood Hills and back into West Hollywood. Then he took me out of West Hollywood and up into the Hollywood Hills again. After a few miles of winding left and right turns, all pretense of following him without detection was gone. We were alone up on the country roads, surrounded by nothing but sage and pine and scrub and dusty rocky hillsides.

I steered the course. The black car was never close, not really. My Buick was a good machine but it was heavy, reinforced to take the weight of its unusual driver and then heavier again with the driver *in situ*. All in all it was slow, but not slower than the black car in front. We were evenly matched.

Ahead he took a bend too fast and the back end fishtailed out, catching in the loose dirt at the side of the tarmac, throwing up a dust storm and a shower of gravel. The gravel had returned to Earth by the time I entered the cloud but the dust was thick and danced in the slipstream of the black car. When I came out the other side the black car was getting smaller on the road ahead.

So I stepped on it. The Buick roared and it seemed to move forward a little faster, but not much.

The telephone next to my hip rang. I kept one hand on the wheel and kept the car pointed at my target as I picked up the receiver with my other hand.

"Now is not the time, Ada."

"You're a robot, Chief. You can multitask now and again. Good for the circuits."

"Uh-huh," I said, pulling tight around a corner and feeling grateful there wasn't traffic coming the other way, the way I had crossed the center line. A robot was liable to have an accident, chasing cars like this.

"I've got the pictures you took outside the house. You're good at portraits, Ray. Nice and clear."

"Thanks," I said, "but you could have complimented me back at the office."

"Now now, Ray. No need to get feisty."

"Sorry." The road began to climb more steeply. We were going up.

"I've got an ID on Charles David's tattooed gardener."

"Really?"

"Really. His name is Artem Rokossovsky."

"Sounds Russian."

"We'll make a detective out of you yet," said Ada. "Rokossovsky is military. Soviet special forces."

"That's some gardener."

"That's not all he is. He's part of an elite unit that was stationed at a place called *Shchyolkovo-14*."

"Sounds nice." I took a left turn too fast and then a right turn not fast enough. Then I came over a rise and saw the black car.

"They also call it Star City," said Ada.

"Sounds nicer. How did you get his info?"

There was a creaking sound like someone leaning back in the office chair and then a squeaking sound like that same chair was being turned around so the person in it could look out the window. I didn't know if those sounds were real or phantoms conjured by my hot transistors.

"A girl has her secrets, Ray. And friends in high places. But the tattoos are like fingerprints. The gardener is Artem Rokossovsky, no question."

"So what is friend Artem doing tending Charles David's roses?"

"Just sit tight and listen hard, Chief," said Ada. "Star City is one big science research complex. Rokossovsky was shipped out there and placed under direct command of one of their top brainboxes. Guy called Vitaly Bobrov. And Bobrov has been on the CIA watch list for a decade now. The U.S. government has even tried to turn him a couple of times, but it never worked."

"So if Artem is here, then maybe his boss is, too?"

"You're on fire today."

"What was Bobrov doing in Star City? The CIA must have targeted him specifically for recruitment."

Ada laughed. I didn't like it.

"You're going to get a kick of this one, Chief."

"Lay it on me."

"Our Vitaly Bobrov is a robotics expert."

Of all the things I had heard today that I didn't like, I didn't like that one the most.

"He was supposedly working on automated systems for Soviet lunar missions," Ada continued. "Star City is the Russian Cape Canaveral. But the CIA thinks his position there was itself a cover."

"So if he wasn't making robots for the moon, what was he doing?"

"That they don't know. But what do you bet it has something to

do with glass cubes that pump out enough energy to kill an unsus-
pecting squirrel at fifty paces?"

The road straightened up as the car crawled on a plateau covered
by forest. It was nice. The light was dappled. It felt cooler.

I slowed and looked around, checking the front, rear, sides. Then
I slowed some more, just coasting along.

"Problem, Ray?"

"I lost the black car."

"Hmm," said Ada. There was a scratching sound. Then there was
a puffing sound and a sniff.

I pulled up under a big old pine with broad, twisted branches
and took another look around. There were plenty of roads leading
off the main strip, most of them just brown dirt. It was the perfect
place to lead a tail and then lose him.

I had to hand it to the guy in the black car—he was good. Whoever he was. Charles David's CIA handler. A Russian agent. Maybe
it was the mysterious Bobrov himself, although if it was then he'd
had lessons in how to shake a tail.

I swapped the phone from one side of my head to the other, like
that would make any difference at all. I sat in the car. I thought and
thought some more.

I wound down the window of the driver's door. The day was getting long. The sound of insects and birds filtered in. It was nice.
I liked it a lot. Maybe I was turning into a country robot.

"Okay," I said. "I'm heading back to town to pay the late Mr. Rockwell a surprise visit."

Then I heard a car coming. I looked in the rearview and saw a
cloud of dust growing at the horizon, where the road came up over
the hill. It got closer. I couldn't see it through the dust. I didn't give
it much thought. It was a free country and I was a robot minding
his own business, talking to his computer boss on a nice sunny
Thursday afternoon.

"Report back as soon as you can, Ray," said Ada. "And be careful."

The car was close now. It was silver. Wide at the front. There was a hood ornament rising from the radiator cap like a gun sight. The car trailed a cloud of light brown dust that lit up in the sun like a comet coming in for a once-in-a-lifetime pass.

"I'll keep an eye out for strange Russian robotics professors, sure."

As I hung up the phone the car pulled up alongside me and stopped. The driver kept the car running as they leaned across the passenger seat and wound down the window. I wound down my window and we stared at each other a while. I was frowning on the inside and the driver of the other car was smiling on the outside. It was a cute smile, the way it made dimples in her cheeks.

"Get in," said Eva McLuckie. "We need to talk."

23

Her car was something European, spacious and well built, with room enough to take my bulk and suspension that didn't protest too much when I got in.

"I'm glad you stopped by," I said, "because I have some questions, and those questions need some answers." I nodded out the windshield. "You can talk and drive at the same time. The Temple of the Magenta Dragon, please. I think you have the address."

Eva McLuckie drove with both hands on the wheel and both eyes on the road. She drove pretty fast but it was steady and it was smooth.

"So where the hell have you been?" I asked. "You were supposed to call the office."

Eva shrugged behind the wheel. "I was busy." Her eyes flicked in my direction, just for a second, before returning to the road ahead. We were nearly off the hills and the traffic was getting thicker. "So consider this my call. What have you got for me? Is the job done?"

I wondered what to tell her. The truth, I supposed. Or at least part of the truth.

In a moment, anyway. My own agenda had one or two action items on it.

"So this case of nervous exhaustion. I understand it's in all the papers. It would be a pretty good cover in case you needed to drop out of sight for a while, right?"

Her grip tightened on the wheel and we picked up just a hint of speed. She didn't seem to want to answer that question, so I tried another one.

"You want to tell me what was going on down in that basement the other night?"

"I don't know," she said.

"You don't know?"

We pulled up at some lights. The car's engine purred smooth as silk somewhere a long way in front of me. Eva took a deep breath and turned to face me.

"Look, metal man, did you do the job or not?"

I looked at her. "Charles David is dead, if that's what you're asking me." I looked at her some more.

The lights changed. Eva McLuckie drove the car. I glanced at her. She was staring at the road. Her nostrils were doing what they did when the person in charge of them was trying to keep calm and suck in enough oxygen to keep the brain going.

"You should be pleased," I said. I raised an eyebrow, or at least it felt like I did. I watched her face but her expression was hard to read. She was holding something in. Holding lots in. I got that. But she was good at controlling it, or hiding it at least.

She was an actor, after all.

"You don't look pleased."

Her lip curled and she let out a big breath. "Why should I be pleased, robot?"

I turned back to admire the front view. "I mean," I said, "I can understand why you did it. Charles David was a double agent and you found out. Then he found out that you found out and he ran. You had to eliminate him before he got back to his handlers and blew the plan your Red friends had concocted wide open." I shrugged.

"You needed someone to find him first, though. You couldn't do it yourself. So you came to me, because you knew I could handle both aspects of the case. How *did* you know, by the way?"

Eva squeezed the steering wheel like she was using it to keep herself upright.

She didn't answer.

"Okay," I said. "Of course I'm wondering why you couldn't just get your friends to help. But I'm guessing that's because you didn't want them to know. You and Charles were partners—a team, maybe. The Russians put you in pairs." I thought about Fresco Peterman and Alaska Gray and liked my theory. "Each responsible for the other, neither able to get direct help from other teams in case it blew the cover. Neat."

We drove on. I watched the traffic.

"But the gold is the really interesting part," I said. "You're a movie star. I imagine you have a bank balance big enough to make grown men weep. But you didn't want to use any of that money to pay me. I get that, too. That could be traced too easily if someone were to get an idea. Instead you used gold. Completely untraceable. Only it wasn't your gold. And I have a feeling the rightful owners weren't too pleased when they found out you'd borrowed it."

Eva licked her lips.

"You know I have a contract to kill you, Ms. McLuckie?"

She might have been shaking or it might have been her holding onto the steering wheel too tightly.

"You're not saying much there, driver."

"You seem to like the sound of your own voice. It seemed rude to interrupt."

I frowned on the inside and turned to watch the streets of Hollywood slip by my window. "Question is, whose gold is it?" The question was directed mostly at myself. "The gold isn't the normal kind. Unmarked ingots, small enough to be transported easily. Say, transported *secretly*. Across borders. Across continents, even." I turned back to Eva. "Say, from Mother Russia? The gold is Soviet. You're working for them and you knew they had it. So when things went slippery with your partner Charles David, it was up to you to fix things. You knew they had the gold, so you took it. That's neat. It doesn't come back to you, and maybe if they found it gone they could pin it on Charles David. All you needed to do was find him and eliminate him before that happened. Present it all wrapped up neat. There was no risk with me on the case. You stuck around a little—long enough to attend the next meeting of your Hollywood Communist club—but then someone noticed the gold was missing and they think you took it. Bam, your plan is history. Now you're on the run from your own people, right? That's quite a situation, I must admit."

Eva didn't say anything but she shook her head a little. I don't know if that meant I was wrong or I was right and she was merely shaking her head in admiration of the deductions my electromatic brain was capable of.

Professor Thornton would have been proud. That I did know.

"Do you know what's going to happen on Friday?" I asked. "Charles David talked about a phase three and a phase four. I assume you know what they are. This is the point where you can start talking, and start talking fast."

That was when Eva pulled to the curb sharply and stopped. She left the engine running and looked at me and then pointed out the window. I turned to look.

We were on Sunset Boulevard. We'd stopped outside a door that was black with a gold number on it and underneath the number was a Chinese character.

I turned back to Eva and she nodded at the door. "Fresco will be inside. He can fill you in on the plan and what we need you to do."

"Me? Have you been listening to a word I've said, lady? I'm not looking to be part of any Soviet master plan."

"You already are," she said. "We all are."

We stared at each other for six and three-quarter seconds. "You're coming in, too," I said. Eva nodded.

I reached for the door handle and opened the door and stepped out. I closed the door.

Then Eva drove off. I frowned on the inside and watched her go.

And then I watched as a black car with soft suspension driven by a man in black hat came down the street and followed her a couple of car lengths back.

I was supposed to kill Eva.

And now I wondered if someone else was going to do the job for me. Her own organization, most likely. They'd used me to find her and now they figured they could finish the job themselves.

Ada wasn't going to like giving them a refund, even a partial one.

I turned to the black door and looked for the handle, but there wasn't one. No bell, no knocker. No window.

Not that any of that mattered when it was opened by a Chinese girl wearing a black silk dress with red trim. She held the door open and she bowed low and gestured for me to enter.

So I did.

24

The Temple of the Magenta Dragon might have looked swell at night with the lights down low and the air full of smoke—I didn't remember of course, I just had Ada's word that I'd been here before—but during the day it was a dump. Every surface was painted black, that kind of flat matte black that the backstage of theaters were painted so they didn't reflect any light. The ceiling was a mess of pipes and buttresses and the walls weren't much better. The black paint made everything look cheap, tacky, especially because the place was lit with harsh fluorescent strip lights that somehow stained the flat black walls a sort of dirty gray. There were no windows. You could lose time in a place like this.

What wasn't black-painted pipework was Chinese decoration. Fake bamboo. Fake clouds. Fake dragons. Under the strip lights they looked rough. Just another set of stage props. Nestled among these disappointing features were other lights set at various angles. Theater lights, their apertures controlled by metal slats, some of them with their bulbs obscured behind what looked like red cellophane. Of course, with the main lights off and the special lights on, the place would look different. The walls and the ceiling would disappear and you'd be in an Oriental wonderland.

Just not before nine p.m.

The main room was filled with round tables and there was a bar on one side. The bar itself was a deep reddish wood, carved in swirls and loops as the contours of an elaborate Chinese dragon took shape. It looked like the bar had been brought in from somewhere else and the surroundings hacked into shape to match this centerpiece.

The far wall was done out in red studded leather and there were some private booths against it, the tables shielded by pierced Chinese folding screens that looked like they could be moved around at will.

There was no sign of the woman who had let me in but at the far end of the bar was another Chinese woman. She was standing behind the bar, her arms folded. She was wearing a sleeveless black tunic with a high collar and had silver bracelets wrapped around her biceps and her hair was pulled back and held in place by some fancy Chinese woodwork. She didn't look amused so I left her to it and headed toward the one booth that was occupied. The man stood up and held his arms out like he was welcoming his new wife home from work.

"Sparks, how you doing? Why don't you come join me, big fella."

Fresco Peterman was wearing a white shirt with the sleeves rolled up and a big dirty napkin tucked into the collar. There was something colorful folded on the seat next to him—it took me a moment to realize it was a casual jacket—and on the table were an open ledger book and a bowl of noodles. The noodles steamed. He had a set of chopsticks in one hand.

I took a seat. Fresco sat down and gestured at his bowl.

"Don't mind if I eat, do you? Bit of a working dinner, you know how it is."

I glanced down at the ledger Fresco had next to his elbow. I didn't need Ada's help to see it was some kind of accounts record, lots of columns of numbers and simple math.

"Doing the books?"

Fresco dabbed his mouth with his napkin. "Gotta keep up with the books."

"You run this place?"

He nodded. "I *own* it. Bit of a hobby, I must admit. Actually, I'm co-owner. One of eight."

I glanced up at the matte black ceiling and the strip light that was directly over our booth. The light was flickering one hundred and twenty times a second, about double the frequency of the main power. To most people it produced nothing but a flat white light. For some people, that flat white light became irritating after a while. That was the flicker. They couldn't *see* it, but it had an effect all the same.

I *could* see the flicker. One twist of my optics and the fluorescent bulb flashed and flashed again like lightning glimpsed beyond a distant horizon. With a little adjustment, I managed to match the flicker of the light with the clicking of my Geiger counter. I returned my attention to the source, which was right in front of me: Fresco Peterman, famous actor, part-time nightclub co-owner.

"It takes eight people to run this joint?" I asked.

Fresco shrugged. "Less for each of us to do. Like I said, it's a hobby. You know this place used to be a fruit market. Pineapples and peaches, can you believe it? On Sunset Boulevard? I mean, come on. Who likes pineapples?"

I couldn't answer that nugget so I didn't. Fresco took my silence as agreement. He nodded and the leather of the booth's bench seat creaked under his famous ass.

"Anyway, we bought it, did it up. Turned it into this little joint."

I looked around again. "Why?"

Fresco cocked his head. "Why?"

"Why a nightclub?" I asked. "Hollywood must be full of them. Who needs another?"

"Ah," said Fresco. He rested his elbows on the table and brought his hands together in a triangle in front of his nose. "Absolutely right, Sparks. But what we needed was a place to call our own. See, those other places, you're always someone's guest, on someone's list, have someone's invite. And as soon as you arrive, people are all over you. All over you!" He chuckled to himself. "Okay, sure, so they're just being nice and doing what they think they should be doing, keeping the rich and famous happy while extracting as much cash out of their wallets as possible. Which is fair enough. Business is business."

"Business is business," I said. I thought Mr. Fresco Peterman and Ada would get along like a house on fire.

Fresco made a clicking sound with his tongue. "Right. So. We opened this place. It's still a club, but one where we control the guest list. It's a place we can come and not worry about anything. We can come and have a drink and not be bothered."

"Or come and get an early dinner on the tab," I said.

Fresco made a pistol shape with his fingers and pointed it at me and mimed his imaginary gun going off.

"There's the detective," he said, his grin picture perfect and worth a thousand bucks to the right buyer. "I knew I liked you. Sci-fi, I'm telling you. Sci-fi." Then he went back to his food.

"I'm here for a reason, Mr. Peterman. I've just been talking to Eva McLuckie."

Fresco pointed his chopsticks at me. "We can count on you for Friday, right?"

I would have raised an eyebrow at that. Honestly, I gave it a good try but it didn't work.

"You're going to need to tell me who 'we' are, and tell me quick."

Fresco nodded and chased noodles in his bowl. He waved his free hand at his jacket.

"Inside pocket," he said as he chewed. His hand kept waving.

I sat and reached around the table and lifted his jacket. I flipped it over, felt a lump in one pocket, and pulled out a big, long wallet. The man watched me and nodded, so I opened the wallet. Inside was a driver's license with his grinning mug shot and the name FRESCO PETERMAN.

So that was his real name. Well I never.

There was also five hundred dollars in hundred-dollar bills and a slim envelope that had already been torn open. I ignored the money and took out the envelope and looked inside.

"Tickets to the *Red Lucky* premiere on Friday," said Fresco. He paused in his mastication. "You *can* come, right? The world isn't going to know what's hit it, Sparks! You just gotta be there, okay?"

Noodles tamed, Fresco laughed and knocked me on the shoulder with his knuckles. Then he winced and shook his hand and flexed his fingers. Then he laughed again.

"You're swell, Sparks," he said. "Real swell." He gestured across the table with his chopsticks. "You and me, we're going to get on just fine. There'll be some important folk there on Friday, too. They're dying to meet you. Dying to."

"Does that include the late, lamented Chip Rockwell?"

Fresco sat back with his chopsticks resting in the bowl and a faint glisten on his chiseled jaw. He ran his fingers through his hair but I didn't see the hair move any and Fresco Peterman didn't seem to notice, either.

Then he nodded, then he clicked his fingers at me and returned his attention to the bowl of noodles.

"So how long have you been a Soviet agent, Mr. Peterman?" I asked, using what we call in the business the direct approach. "And tell me, how much does the KGB have to pay to buy a movie star's loyalty? Must be steep. You must be richer than your friend Charles David, and I've seen his house."

Fresco's eyes narrowed a little as he looked at me over his bowl. His appetite seemed to be diminishing by the moment. I worked to diminish it further.

"Did you know your buddy was working for the opposition? He was about to bust you wide open."

Fresco smiled a sickly smile and he spread his arms wide as he sat back in the booth. "I don't see Charles David anywhere," he said.

"Charles David might not be here, but I am."

"And I suppose that's supposed to frighten me, Sparks, is that it?" The smile stayed just where it was on Fresco's face.

My turn to shrug. "Can't say I care one way or the other. But I'm going to take a look in your basement. That's where you keep Rockwell, right? In fact, that's why you and your friends bought this place, isn't it? A private place to gather with a cellar just right for a good-sized secret or two."

Something strange happened to Fresco's face. His smile froze and his expression became as solid as his hair. He clenched his hands and I could see his finger joints go white as he squeezed.

I think he was thinking.

"Fine, let's talk," he said, and he flicked his head like he was trying to shake it without shaking it. The smile was still fixed over all those Hollywood teeth. "Friday. Phase three. I need you to be ready."

I shook my head. "Tell me about Chip Rockwell. Last chance before I go take a look for myself."

Fresco didn't say anything.

"Okay," I said. "I'll just call the police and then we're going to take a little look in your basement."

"Wait," said Fresco. "Fine. You want to look in the basement, you look in the basement." Fresco stood. "Hey! Rico! Get over here."

I turned on the seat as three men came out of a door by the bar.

All three of them I recognized from the secret meeting, thanks to Ada's helpful playback of my memory tape.

Parker Silverwood. Bob Thatcher. And in front, Rico Spillane. Three actors, A-list movie stars.

Three lieutenants of the Soviet cell.

"Rico," said Fresco. "Show Sparks around. Give him the tour." He turned back to me. "You're my guest. Just promise me you'll be ready Friday. I need you to be there, okay?"

I didn't answer his question. Instead I looked Rico up and down and left and right.

"You feeling better then, Mr. Spillane? Re-transfer good for the soul, right?"

Rico Spillane said not a word. Instead he jerked his head sideways, which I took to be an invitation.

I stood and walked toward the door by the bar. I didn't wait to see if my escort was following.

25

Two hours later I stepped out onto Sunset Boulevard. The black door of the Temple of the Magenta Dragon closed behind me with barely a click.

The basement was a bust, of course. Cleared out. Not even the big round table was down there. Rico and Parker and Bob had given me full access, opening any and every door. But they hadn't spoken a word once.

Which was fine by me because I was busy listening to my Geiger counter and it had quite the story to tell. Whatever had been in the basement—Chip Rockwell, or what was left of him—had left a hot trail, one that ended in a loading bay out of the back of the club. I had stood there with Rico and Parker and Bob and kept my thoughts to myself.

When we got back up top, Fresco was gone. The nice Chinese lady let me out. I looked down the street and then I looked up it, and then I remembered my car was still up on a country lane several miles out of town.

And Eva McLuckie? Who knew.

I frowned on the inside and eyed the pay phone on the corner. I should have called Ada. Given her an update. Let her know what I was up to.

But I wanted to move, and move fast. I wasn't sure how long the heat of my new trail was going to last.

So instead I looked around and got my bearings and turned my Geiger counter up. It began a steady tick and I began to follow the breadcrumbs.

Radioactive breadcrumbs.

I found my way around the block and followed the trail a few yards until I could see the back of the club and the roller door of its loading bay. Then I turned around and followed the trail back up the street the other way.

Chip Rockwell was on the move.

And I was on his tail.

I walked for a while. I ignored most people around me and most did the same. That was fine. More than fine. I wished them all happy lives in which they could ignore me at their leisure.

I just hoped those happy lives extended beyond Friday night.

At intersections cars came and went and some drivers slowed to look at me as they cruised around the corner and one, a young man in a tight white T-shirt, even leaned on the horn as he did so. But he gave me a cheery wave out the window as his tires squealed and I waved back and he seemed happy enough.

I kept on walking and kept on following the crackle in my head. It came and went—they'd moved Chip in a vehicle from the loading dock, that much was obvious, and the trail they left went through peaks and troughs that probably matched the ebb and flow of traffic.

That traffic was particularly bad this evening, thanks to the lane

closure right outside a red, green, and gold–colored fake temple that
I soon found myself standing outside.

Grauman's Chinese Theatre. Where the curtain would go up on
the premiere of *Red Lucky* in about twenty-four hours.

I checked the Geiger and checked it again.

The theater was red hot.

Chip Rockwell was inside.

There was a phone booth a couple of doors down and it started to
ring. I walked up to it and stood half-in, half-out of the booth. They
weren't made for mechanical men of my dimensions.

"Enjoying the sights and sounds of Hollywood, Ray?"

"Hello, Ada."

Ada took a sip of something she couldn't possibly be drinking.
"You know we still have two payments to go."

I pulled the phone's heavy metal cord a little between two
steel fingers and turned to look down the street back toward the
theater.

"Two payments on what?"

Ada sighed. "The *car*, Ray. I sure hope you didn't leave the keys
in it."

I patted my pocket. They keys were there.

"It's fine," I said. "I'll pick it up later. Listen to this."

I filled her in and when I was done she whistled.

"Great," said Ada. "So Charles David was working for the CIA
and he wanted to kill you. Fresco Peterman works for the KGB and
he wants you for the mysterious phases three and four. Hey, maybe
I could hire you out? How much would you say the rental is on a
robot like your good self?"

"Ada!"

She laughed inside my head. "Tuxedos. Vintage dresses. Killer
robots. What's the difference, Ray?"

I ignored her and kept my optics on the theater. It was closed. It shone in the last light of sunset. It had had a fresh coat of paint.

Ready for the premiere.

"It's all going down on Friday," I said. "The movie premiere."

"Phase three."

I nodded. "And I'm phase four, apparently."

"Makes you wonder what phases one and two were."

I shrugged. "You and me both." I stood there and listened to the hiss on the phone and the cars on the street. "What do you want me to do about Eva, in case I see her again?"

"Well, we've been paid in full, Ray. I'd hate to have to give that money back."

"No luck with the client, then?"

"Nope," said Ada. "But I think you're right and it's the Russians wanting to take her out for stealing their gold."

"Couldn't they have done that themselves? I would assume a simple hit on one of their own agents would be a pretty easy job."

"Why don't you ask your old pal Chip when you see him? Anyway, she'd taken off. They needed someone to find her first."

"I don't like the idea of working for the Soviet Union."

"Says Mr. Phase Four."

I shook my head. "Charles David said we had to stop phase three first. And I'm starting to feel that's a pretty good idea."

"So what are you going to do about this feeling, Chief?"

I looked at the theater. While I was looking it sounded like Ada put something down on the desk in the office. I wondered idly what I would find out if I did a reverse directory on the calls.

I wondered idly if I did that every day and never remembered the answer.

Then that sound was gone and all that was left was a ticking sound. It wasn't the Geiger counter this time. This was the sound of a watch, a small pocket watch, the second hand racing ever onward.

It was the sound of the computer room back at the office.

The sound of Ada's heartbeat.

"Mission control to Raymond Electromatic, come in, please," said Ada.

"Sorry," I said. "I was just thinking."

"Tell me about it."

"It's time I spoke to Chip Rockwell."

"Just don't forget to buy a ticket before you go in, Ray."

I smiled on the inside. I hung up.

I walked up the block to the Chinese Theatre.

26

The lights were on inside the theater but the main doors were locked. There was a sign on those locked doors with one arrow pointing to the box office and another pointing in the opposite direction suggesting that contractors use the tradesmen's entrance. There was a second sign next to the first, hand-lettered on a big white card, to say the place would be closed until next week due to Friday's "nationwide gala premiere of motion-picture history, *Red Lucky.*"

I tried the doors again but they just rattled like they'd rattled the first time. Only now the noise had caught the attention of a man in a flat cap and denim overalls with a white T-shirt underneath the straps and a thick mustache under his nose. He was walking from my left across the theater lobby, carrying something long and wrapped in a painted-spattered cream cloth on his shoulder.

He stopped and looked at me. Then he rebalanced the object on his shoulder and walked up to the doors. He looked at me some more. I looked back, and touched the brim of my hat in greeting. The man jerked to life and leaned his cargo against the wall and then fussed with the door from his side. There was a hearty *thunk* as he twisted the lock and a squeak as he pulled the door open just a crack.

He nodded at me through the crack, his eyes seeming to rest on my hat rather than my optics. The mustache didn't suit him. It made him look older than he probably was. And he needed a haircut. I kept these thoughts to myself.

"Hi," he said, in a tone that suggested saying hello to a robot had brightened his day a little. "Can I help you, man? Just the theater is closed, y'know, for the premiere."

I reached into my jacket, took out the wallet with the badge in it, and opened it to show him. He nodded as he looked at it and straightened up. With one hand he adjusted the cloth-covered object he'd leaned against the wall and with the other he opened the door a little wider. I wasn't just anyone walking in off the street, after all. I was a robot detective on a case. He seemed real eager to cooperate.

"Oh, so, man, what's up? Anything I can do to help"—he slapped his thigh—"I'm your man. Name is Jake, but you can call me Sparks."

I smiled at this. He didn't see it, of course.

"Electrician, huh?" I asked.

He nodded.

"Listen Sparks, I'm working for Mr. Fresco Peterman," I said. That wasn't true but Sparks seemed to like what I was saying so I kept on saying it. "I was just in the neighborhood, thought I'd take a look at the theater. Just a preliminary check, you know how it is. A quick sweep and I'll be out of your hair."

Sparks nodded. Then he looked over his shoulder. The theater lobby was covered in as much gold and green and red as the outside of the place. I thought then I knew where Fresco had got his interior design ideas from.

Sparks turned back and nodded again. "Okay, you wanna come in and wait, man, no problem, no problem at all." He jerked a thumb over one shoulder. "I'd better just go get Walter. He's the manager. He'll be looking after everyone, y'know, on Friday, too. Wait here, I'll go get him."

I nodded and lifted my hat and Sparks jogged away from me. Then he stopped and turned and clicked his fingers in my direction. "Fresco Peterman?" Then he slapped a leg and said, "Wow-whee!" in a way that sounded like he meant it, and then he was gone.

I turned back to the doors. I looked out of them. Then I twisted the big lock home. Didn't want just anyone wandering in, after all.

I heard footsteps and a telephone rang somewhere and some people called out somewhere else. The lobby might have been empty but it sounded like Friday's crew was still prepping the theater.

I turned my Geiger counter up and used it like a compass to get a nuclear-powered bearing.

I waited a few minutes. Walter was clearly a busy man. I stood there and thought about what I would say and what I would ask and then I thought I probably didn't want to speak to him at all, seeing as I didn't work for Fresco Peterman and I wasn't here to check on security arrangements for Friday. Every A-lister in town would be standing in this lobby in just over twenty-four hours and chances were Walter knew exactly what the security arrangements were— and how they most certainly didn't involve a robot pretending to be a PI.

The telephone kept ringing and the people kept calling out and I slipped over to the doors to the main auditorium, cracked them open, and slipped inside.

I wasn't sure what I expected to find inside the auditorium. I was standing at the back, looking out over a sea of red velvet seats with gold woodwork, the whole thing sloping gently toward the stage. I didn't know how many people could worship the silver screen in one sitting but it looked like an awful lot.

The walls were gold and red as well and I had to admit they were something else. They showed friezes of woodland scenes separated by great gold columns. The ceiling right over my head was the floor of the circle above and from it hung great gold chandeliers shaped like Chinese lanterns. Beyond, the ceiling vanished into the stratosphere in order for the auditorium to accommodate what was clearly a very large screen indeed, hidden behind the red curtains that continued the Oriental forest theme in elaborate gold embroidery.

It seemed like a nice place to hold a film premiere.

I was alone in the auditorium. There didn't seem to be much to set up in here, after all. The curtains were closed. The lights were on but their glow was swallowed by the soft velvet depths of the place. As I walked forward my footfalls sounded dull and far away underneath the ever-increasing rattle of my radiation detector. The acoustics in the place were impressive.

I turned around to get the full view. There was a big star-shaped chandelier right in the middle of the high ceiling and what I'd thought was the circle was actually a couple of boxes flanking the windows of the projection room.

There were a couple of people in one of the boxes. One was bent over a chair and was hammering something. The other had his back to me.

I didn't want Walter to find me and I didn't want the two workmen to see me so I tap-danced down the aisle and found an unmarked black door next to the stage.

Chip Rockwell was close.

I let myself through.

Backstage at Grauman's reminded me some more of the Temple of the Magenta Dragon. Out of public view, the whole place was an endless matte black that did strange things to the light and it had a smell that was like the inside of a hot air cupboard.

I tiptoed down a few tight corridors. There was nobody around but I could hear hammering and voices from somewhere.

And, in the darkness, the pop and fizz of my Geiger counter. The signal got louder and denser the farther I went, so I went farther. After only a short time I came to a set of short black steps that led up into a black space lit by a pale light that had a greenish tint.

I went up the steps and found myself in the wings at the back of the stage. About twenty yards to my right was the actual back of the silver screen. It shone in the dim light like quicksilver.

The screen only got some cursory attention. What really caught my eye was the machinery behind it.

It was black metal, and lots of it, all girders and struts arranged into a series of sharp angles. At first I thought it was a scaffold, something temporary or maybe even permanent to allow staff up to the back of the screen or to something equally high. I looked up and there was nothing there. No lighting rig. No high-altitude walkways and ladders hanging from chains from the ceiling like you might find in other theaters.

The big metal thing had a disk on the front of it and that disk was pointed at the back of the movie screen. The disk, like the screen, was silver. It was twenty yards in diameter and in the center was a pointed cone, the point aimed at the movie screen's bull's-eye.

I moved again, looking up.

Behind the big disk was a fat cylinder, from which sprouted cables that were fixed to the scaffold by metal straps and led away down to the floor and then down the steps on the opposite side of the stage. The fat cylinder had a curved rear end and there was a protuberance sticking out of the back, like the end of an axle.

Which is just what it was. The fat cylinder was a motor. The big silver disk was built to turn.

I didn't know what it was but I knew it wasn't the kind of standard equipment you'd find in a movie theater. Maybe it was part of the fancy new transmission system, the exciting wizardry that was going to beam every frame of *Red Lucky* straight into cinemas all over the country.

Or at least that's what I would have thought, had it not been identical in every way but scale to the gadget I'd found in the honeymoon suite of the Ritz-Beverly Hotel.

The greenish tint to the light backstage was cast by a green light on the side of the machine's base, next to a control panel. I looked it over and took some readings from my Geiger counter. They were high, but this wasn't the source. As with Fresco and Eva, the thing had been exposed to radioactive material but was not itself radioactive.

The source being Chip Rockwell.

I checked my bearings and then looked at the fat cable coming out of the bottom of the control box. It was heading off in the right direction, so I decided to follow it.

27

I followed the cable all the way to the roof, my Geiger counter in complete agreement. On the way I'd only had to hide twice to avoid workmen. The place felt like everything was ready and there was just a skeleton crew left to tidy up. I didn't know what had happened to Sparks and his boss Walter. Maybe Walter had told him to get back to work after Sparks had told him there was a robot in a hat waiting for him in the lobby and they'd gone to the lobby and found nothing.

That didn't bother me.

What did bother me was what the cable led to on the roof, and what that was was certainly not Chip Rockwell. It was another disk fitted to another machine. This setup was smaller than the one downstairs but bigger than the one on the dental chair rig at the hotel. The disk of this one was maybe six feet across and it was pointing at the Hollywood Hills.

More specifically, it was pointed at something *on* the hills. It was getting dark and as I stood on the roof and watched the dusk settle like a foggy blanket I saw the whole show.

First it lit up **HOLLY**.

Then it lit up **WOOD**.

Then it lit up **HOLLYWOOD**. And if you hadn't got the idea yet, **HOLLYWOOD** flashed twice more before the cycle started again.

Ada had told me about what I'd found up there. The sign hadn't been lit in more than forty years. And all this in honor of the *Red Lucky* premiere. They'd done a good job.

Why the disk of the rooftop machine was pointed at the Hollywood Sign, I didn't know. It all had something to do with the transmission. Nationwide, a hundred theaters, *Red Lucky* beamed into every one of them.

The transmission.

Phase three.

"Okay, hold it right there."

I froze. I stared at the Hollywood Sign. I wondered whether I should put my hands up or not. Then I tried to think of any gun I knew short of a howitzer that could actually scratch my chassis. I came up blank, so I just stood there and left my hands right where they were.

"Turn around," said the man's voice. "Slowly," he added. They always tell you to do it slowly. Sensible enough, I supposed.

I obliged the man and turned on my heel. He was standing by the side of the stairwell block, a silhouette against a sky that was a bruised orange purple. His outline was that of a man in a hat and a long coat. He had that hat on at an angle you might call jaunty—if the guy wearing it wasn't holding a gun on you.

I took one look at the gun he was holding and revised my list of dangerous weapons. I decided to hold my hands up after all.

The gun was silvery and shaped like a pinecone, with a body that looked like it was made out of blown glass and that came to a point rather than the usual kind of open barrel. There was some business inside the blown-glass body but I couldn't see any details and I wasn't in the mood to zoom in. Behind the body was a grip the man held like a regular pistol and there was a trigger he had his finger on.

I'd never seen anything like it. It looked very interesting and very dangerous at the same time.

As I stood in the dusk-light on that rooftop I considered the strange gun and considered that it was clearly the kind of gun that was made for just this sort of occasion and for just this kind of target.

That target being me. A robot. The last one.

"Don't move," said the man.

"Do I look like I'm moving?"

The man waved the gun. Changeable fellow, but I took the hint and I sidestepped away from the machine on the roof while the man sidestepped toward it. When we'd completed one half turn of this circular dance he quickly glanced at the machine and then he looked back at me.

"I didn't touch your machine," I said. "I was just taking a look."

The man glanced back at the contraption and his eyes stayed there for a moment. The way they moved over the object told me all I needed to know: he knew even less about it than I did.

"So, you going to tell me what this is about?" I asked.

The man's attention returned to me and he frowned. He began to move sideways, back toward the stairs. He kept the gun on me and I kept my front to him.

"Because," I said, "you've been following me all over town. And not very well, either. I mean, you're a good driver but that car sticks out like a sore thumb. You want to tail someone, you need to blend right in."

"Of course," said the man, "and you'd know all about that, wouldn't you, Detective?"

He knew I was a detective. Didn't mean a thing. I was the last robot and if people knew about me then they knew I was a detective. That was the cover story. Said very much the same in gold lettering on the door of my office.

I gave a noncommittal shrug with my hands still up around my ears. "You're Charles David's handler. From the Agency. Right?"

"I'm Special Agent Daley. Touch Daley."

"My condolences."

He ignored me. "I've been wanting to talk to you for quite a while, machine man."

"I know the feeling," I said. "You'll be wanting to know what happened to your asset."

"Asset?"

"Sure. Charles David. Movie star. Part-time CIA agent. Tell me, I thought you fellas weren't supposed to operate on American soil?"

"I don't know what you're talking about."

"Oh," I said. "Well, in that case, you should have called my office. I have a secretary. You could have left a message instead of trailing me all over town."

Daley chuckled, and by chuckled I mean his upper body convulsed just once and one side of his mouth went up. It mirrored the dip of his hat brim on the other side.

"Of course," he said. "Ada the miraculous supercomputer." He waved the gun. "I'm not sure she'd like to be called your secretary, though."

This was a new one. That I was supposedly a detective was a matter of public record, if anyone cared to look me up. But this guy, he knew Ada. Nobody knew Ada except me. And . . .

The government.

Oh.

I lifted my steel chin. Touch Daley watched me.

"So you're not CIA. Which department, then?" I asked.

The special agent's chin went up, his posture matching mine. "I'm afraid that's classified."

Huh.

"But you know about me, and about Ada," I said. "So what do you want to talk to me about? I really want it to be about a little cell of Soviet secret agents operating in this fair city, but so far I'm not hopeful."

Daley cocked his head. "Sounds like a handful."

"I sense a *but* coming."

Agent Daley lifted that chin of his again. "Not my department."

"Like you said," I said. "And that department would be . . . ?"

He ignored me. "There was a break-in at a locked-down government research facility recently. Some equipment was stolen. Very advanced, very specialized, very heavy equipment."

I would have frowned if I'd been able to. Instead I said, "And?"

"The facility was run by one Professor C. Thornton, PhD. You may remember him."

I shrugged again. "If you know about me and Ada, then you know about Thornton. You're telling me you trailed me all over town just to ask me if I knew my own creator?"

Daley smiled under his hat. His lips were thin. "Thornton's laboratory has been sealed ever since the prof disappeared three years ago."

This was news to me. I said as much and I asked the reason, too.

"A radiation leak," the agent told me. "The whole place is red hot."

This was also news to me. There seemed to be a lot of radiation in this town. Too much to be coincidental.

Daley cocked his head. "To go in there you'd need to have a death wish. Or . . ."

"Or not be bothered about radiation and strong enough to carry something heavy out," I said. "I get it. But it wasn't me."

At least I didn't think it was. I really didn't know. Was there something Ada hadn't told me? Maybe that explained why Agent Daley here hadn't called the office. He didn't want to talk to Ada, which meant he didn't want Ada to know he was talking to me.

"You wouldn't happen to know anything about the prof's disappearance, now would you?"

I frowned, or at least it felt like I did on the inside. From Agent Daley's point of view I was as still as a statue.

"Can't honestly say," I said honestly.

Agent Daley's eyes narrowed and I thought he might have tightened his grip on his special gun but it was hard to tell so I turned up my optics. When I saw what was behind Agent Daley I still didn't speak, though I knew what was about to happen.

Out of the shadows of the stairwell block a smaller person appeared, lifting something rectangular and heavy up over their head before bringing it down in one quick movement on the back of the agent's neck. Daley dropped the gun first, his fingers opening like a man dropping a cobra, then he groaned and hit the deck. His hat lifted off his head and landed gently beside his body.

Eva McLuckie panted heavily, her feet planted in a wide V, her upper body limp from the waist, her arms hanging. The quarter of a cinder block was still held in both hands and she let it fall to the roof with a *clink*.

I lowered my hands. I opened and closed the steel fingers of both steel hands. They made a clinking sound not entirely unlike the sound the cinder block had made when it hit the roof. Eva McLuckie took a deep breath and she looked up at me. Her eyes seemed to light up from the depths of her dark makeup.

"Aren't you going to say thanks?" she asked.

"Thanks," I said. I moved forward and so did she, kneeling down to feel the side of the agent's neck.

"He'll live," she said, and then she moved quicker than I did and scooped up the agent's weird gun. I didn't say anything. She held it with her fingers around the bulb-shaped body, which hadn't even cracked when it had been dropped. She didn't seem to be interested in pointing it at me.

My logic gates flipped. My processors spun. My electromatic brain sparked. I crunched numbers like a kid crunching cornflakes in front of Saturday morning cartoons.

I waved at the slowly breathing body on the ground between us. "You know this guy?"

"Never seen him," said Eva. She slipped the gun into the pocket of her red coat and then walked over to the machine that was pointing at the Hollywood Sign and she looked in the same direction.

I watched her.

"Where's Chip Rockwell?" I asked.

She turned around.

She said, "Let me show you something."

She walked to the stairs.

And dammit if I didn't just turn and follow her.

28

We drove through the streets of Hollywood in her big silver car. She had that look again, that posture, leaning forward in the driver's seat, balancing on the edge, both hands on the wheel. She turned the wheel slowly, this way and that, this way and that, working just to keep the boatlike car going in a straight line down Sunset Boulevard.

We had left the theater behind us. The clicking of my Geiger counter faded away like smoke drifting from a chimney. Wherever she was taking me it was apparently away from Chip Rockwell.

The lights of Hollywood streamed past in the windows. We made good time. Good time to where, I didn't know.

I thought of the job I was contracted to do. I thought of the different ways I could kill her. It would be easy.

Except I had no intention of carrying out the job. Eva McLuckie had said she wanted to show me something and I wanted to see what that something was. I wanted to know what was going on. I wanted to know what the Soviets were planning.

I wanted to know what had happened to Chip Rockwell.

I glanced at Eva as she drove and saw she was smiling now but the smile was fake and unmoving and didn't turn on those famous dimples that made hearts pound and movie audiences swoon the world over.

Killing her would be easy. So very, very easy.

"I suppose you're asking yourself whether Charles David ever got back to his people," I said. "Considering you and your buddies are part of a Soviet cell determined to disrupt America, I mean. Sounds like a lot of work. Would be a shame for the U.S. government to take an interest."

I thought about the agent from that very same government we'd left unconscious on the rooftop. He didn't fit into the picture. He wasn't interested in Soviet infiltration of the Hollywood movie business. He was interested in me and Ada and Professor Thornton.

I had to tell Ada about this other agent, and soon. But at the moment we had something else to worry about.

Phase three. *Red Lucky*.

I turned in the passenger seat to ask Eva about that but then I saw she was trying very hard to suppress something that was either a howling gale of laughter or an awful lot of tears or maybe even both at once.

"I'm not a Communist," she said. "You were right about Chuck being my partner. I'm working with the CIA. We both were."

She took her eyes off the road for longer than I felt comfortable with and she looked at me and she said, "*We* are trying to stop *them*."

I looked back at her and I wished as hard as I could that she would look where she was driving us. Eventually she did and I let out a breath I didn't even know I was able to hold.

"And you couldn't have told me this earlier because . . . ?"

Eva slapped the steering wheel. "*Goddammit!* Charles was my *partner,* don't you get that, machine man? A partner I had to have *killed* to stop him breaking our cover." She hissed and shook her head. "So you'll forgive me if I've been a little . . . I don't know, *reticent*." She served that last word up with a healthy side of sarcasm. "This is difficult, dammit," she said. "This whole thing is difficult. I've had to do things—make decisions—I will never be able to live with."

I didn't say anything.

She said, "I don't expect a robot to understand."

Was she telling the truth now? I thought about the basement meeting I'd been an eyewitness to, though I didn't remember it.

"If you want me to believe that, then you're going to have to explain a great deal more about what you and Charles were doing. Remember, I saw you at the Temple. You and the others. You were all speaking with Russian accents."

Eva didn't answer straight away. When she did, I didn't like it.

"I don't remember," she said.

"You don't remember what?"

"The basement. I don't remember the meeting."

"Don't tell me—nervous exhaustion?"

I watched the road. We'd been driving a while and it felt like most of that driving had been in circles. Eva was making sure we weren't being followed.

"So what happened to Charles David?" I asked.

Eva shook her head. "Charles was a good agent, but he cracked under the pressure. Things weren't right—I don't know what it was, but he started questioning everything we were doing. Then it got worse, he started with these theories and ideas. The wrong ones. By the end he accused me of collaborating with the enemy—not as a double agent, but like they'd somehow 'got' to me. He was getting out of control."

"And then he vanished."

"Yes," she said, and then Eva looked at me. Her big eyes were wide. The black rings around them made them look bigger. "I had to find him. He was going to blow everything. Months of work. The safety of our nation was at stake."

She turned back to the road ahead.

"I had no choice," she said. Then she wiped a tear from one eye and didn't say any more and she kept driving.

I sat in the passenger seat with a bunch of ideas. I guess I believed Eva, but the more I thought about the contract that had been taken out on her, the less it made sense. If they—the Soviets—had suspected Eva of being an enemy agent, one who had borrowed their stash of untraceable gold, then they could have found her and taken her out themselves, surely? My profession and the skill set that went with it were hardly unique.

But no, they had come to *me*.

I thought about Artem Rokossovsky, the Russian agent posing as Charles David's gardener. If he was in the United States, then it was not unreasonable to assume his boss, Vitaly Bobrov, was here, too.

Bobrov.

The *robotics* expert.

Oh.

That's why they had come to me. Two birds with one stone, perhaps. I could find the girl and their gold, and they would know exactly where I was and what I was doing. And they wanted a tab on me because I was part of their plan. I was, in point of fact, phase four.

I would have frowned if I could have, honest to God. Instead I turned to face Eva. The seat leather underneath me creaked.

"Phase three is the transmission of *Red Lucky*," I said. "But tell me about phase four. Do you even know what it is?"

"No," said Eva with a shake of her head that swung her bangs side to side. "I don't know anything about it, other than the fact that you play a starring role."

"So I've been told. Don't tell me—that's why you came to me about the problem of Charles David. Sure, you needed to find and remove him, but you needed to keep your own eyes on me."

Eva nodded. "But whatever phase four is, phase three is the more urgent problem."

"Charles David told me to stop phase three. So again, what is it, apart from a movie show? It has something to do with the transmission."

We took a left. Then we took a right.

"Yes," Eva said. "A simultaneous transmission, nationwide." She sighed again and shook her head. "Those clever, clever bastards."

We were out of Hollywood now and crawling up the hills. The car slowed as the road began to wind.

"Simultaneous transmission of what?" I asked. I thought about the big machine behind the cinema screen at Grauman's, and I thought about the smaller version of the same on the roof. I thought about the way it was pointed at the Hollywood Sign.

Then the car yawed. Eva McLuckie groaned and slumped right over the wheel. Her hands stayed where they were but their grip was loose and she planted her face in the middle of the wheel.

The car moved to the left, quickly. I reached over and corrected just as fast. The car jerked as Eva's feet slid off the accelerator and onto the brake and then off of it. We began to coast. Given we were pointing uphill, that wasn't going to work. We began to slow. We were going to go backward pretty soon. I looked around but couldn't see any kind of hand brake. It must have been over on the other side, out of my reach.

"Eva! Come on, wake up now!" I guessed that the shock of everything had finally hit her, right at the wrong moment.

Then she jerked her head up and took a whoop of breath, and jerked her head again as she realized she was in charge of a car. She elbowed my arm and gasped in pain as her bones rolled against hard metal. The jab didn't do anything to move my arm of course, but I took my hands away from the wheel and gave her some space.

Back in control, she slid her hands around the wheel and then changed gear and we were on our way again. I turned in the passenger seat. There were headlights coming up behind. We were lucky they were pretty far away and the road was mostly ours. The hillside we were on the side of was steep and I didn't much like the idea of the car going over it. I would probably be okay but I didn't think Eva would fare so well.

Then Eva spoke. To my audio receptors it sounded something like "*Shto ty dielaesh'?*" and there was a rising intonation at the end, so I guessed it was a question.

Then again, I didn't speak Russian.

Eva turned her head to look at me. She had a lip curled in disgust and the dimples were long gone. She seemed to be holding her forehead in a completely different way from before, if that was even possible.

It was like there was someone else behind the wheel now.

Someone who wasn't Eva McLuckie.

"*Derr'mo!*" she said.

I watched her. She even drove differently—she held her hands lower down and she'd sunk back into the seat, giving up the birdlike perch on the edge that Eva had preferred.

And then a telephone rang.

I glanced into the well between the passenger seat and the driver where I had expected the hand brake to be. It still wasn't there. There wasn't a telephone there either, not like in my car.

Russian Eva growled. It was deep in her throat and when I looked at her again her eyes were narrow as she drove. She—whoever she was—was annoyed. I didn't blame her. I knew what it was like to wake up with no idea where you were or what you were doing. Occupational hazard for a robot. Less so for a person, I would have said, at least until now.

The telephone kept ringing. The sound was coming from the dash, right in front of me.

Glove compartment.

I reached for it and Eva reached for it too, but I was closer and got there first and all she could do was slap my hand before returning her own to the wheel. She said something in Russian, pretty loud. She was not a happy customer.

My own patience was starting to run thin, too.

I put the telephone against the side of my head. The glove box lid hung on its hinge, bouncing as we cruised up the hillside. The telephone in my car was a special feature, which meant the telephone in this car was, too. It was just in a different place, built into the glove box to be more discreet when you were a double agent gadding about town.

"Hello?" I said into the receiver. I had a fair idea who it was but I second-guessed myself at the last minute and thought I'd better check it was for me. That would have been embarrassing.

"Your dinner is getting cold and I've let the cat out for the night."

I turned to Eva. She was half-watching me, half-watching the road as she wound the car up like a tightly coiled spring.

"I'm in the middle of something of a situation here, Ada."

"You and me both, Chief," said Ada. "I got a bead on the client who took a professional dislike to Eva McLuckie. Took a lot of digging through sham corporations and overseas accounts, but I got there in the end."

I wished that Ada would program herself a sense of urgency. It might come in useful sometimes. Like now.

"Ada," I said. "I'm in a car with Eva. Only I'm not sure she's driving."

"You mean you're driving from the passenger seat? That's some trick, Ray. You should work in movies."

"I'm just along for the ride, trust me. Who's the client?"

"You're not going to like it," said Ada.

"Try me."

"Vitaly Bobrov."

"I had a feeling."

"It all goes back to him, Chief. He's got funding. Lots of funding."

I lowered the telephone and looked at Eva and she snarled and muttered something under her breath. Inside my head Ada laughed.

I lifted the telephone back up. "Oh, such language," she said. "And I thought she was such a nice girl."

"I think I've worked out why Eva doesn't remember the meeting in the basement."

"Because sometimes she's not Eva, right?"

"Right. So Bobrov has backing. Government backing, right?"

"Feels like it," said Ada. There was a sound, like she'd got up out of a big office chair and was walking around the desk in hard shoes. Then there was the sound of paper shuffling, like she was going through a pile of notes.

At least that's what I thought I heard but I couldn't really be sure so I ignored it.

"So that clinches it," I said. "Bobrov is here and he's here on business."

"And we know what that business is, Ray," said Ada.

"Phase three," I said, "to be followed in short order by phase four."

"We have to stop them, Ray."

"Working on it," I said. I put the phone back in the glove box. I was careful to keep the coiled cord straight but it tangled anyway. I pressed the glove box closed but the catch didn't stick the first time so I pressed it again. Then it stayed put.

Somehow we were still curling up the Hollywood Hills. The car pushed around the next bend and finally the Hollywood Sign came into view. It was big and bright, the sequence of flashing bulbs guaranteeing a bad night's sleep for anyone living within view.

I turned to Russian Eva. I didn't know what to say but it turned out that she wanted to speak first anyway and what she said was,

"Don't try anything," in an accent that was fairly heavy. Like we were back in the basement, when she and her Russian friends had been forced to speak English for someone else's benefit. For someone who was there but didn't speak Russian.

Someone like Chip Rockwell, perhaps.

She had one hand on the wheel and the other was holding the gun Touch Daley had dropped. It was pointed in my direction.

I frowned on the inside and I didn't try a single thing.

29

It had gotten cold up on the hills. That didn't bother me, but I pulled the belt of my trench coat a bit tighter anyway and pushed my hat down about as far as it would go. I couldn't tell whether Russian Eva was bothered by it. She had a face like a storm and she kept pushing the Egyptian bangs that belonged to someone else out of her eyes with the hand that wasn't holding Daley's special gun.

We'd parked in a dirt lot surrounded by a chain-link fence. There was a hut in the lot made of corrugated steel. It had three small, dark windows in the side facing us. The lot and the hut were on a flat piece of ground that had been cut into the hillside. Over the lip of the plateau were some tall structures of metal and wood that were blasted into sharp relief as four thousand lightbulbs on the front of them blazed their infinitely repeating sequence.

We were behind the Hollywood Sign. I had a terrible feeling of déjà vu that I wasn't sure was a genuine memory fragment or me just expecting there to be one.

A moment later my memory tape wound on and the feeling was gone.

We walked down to the sign via a steep and dusty path. Russian Eva was behind me. At the sign itself there was just enough space to walk around in front and behind without taking a tumble down to Hollywood. The hills in front of us were dark shapes punctuated with a scattering of lights, some bright but most faint. Beyond that, Hollywood and the suburbs of Los Angeles were a matrix of yellow and white and red lights. It looked a little like a printed circuit. I tried to pick out the roof of Grauman's Chinese Theatre but everything was as far away as another galaxy.

I turned around to face my captor. Russian Eva seemed as entranced by the view as I was. The gun was still pointing in my direction but there was little effort in it. I didn't know if it was the breeze or something else, but the possessed movie star was swaying on her feet.

"Eva?"

She coughed and looked at me and blinked and coughed again. The gun arm went down.

"We're here," she said in a voice that was most certainly hers.

"What the hell happened?"

Eva pushed the bangs to one side and rubbed her forehead. Her eyes closed in the middle of those big black rings of makeup and they stayed closed. She looked a little spooky at night.

"I'm sorry," she said. She winced. I took a step forward then stood still. "It's hard to fight it," she said. "The drugs help, but they become less effective over time. At least that's what it feels like."

Then she sat down, quickly. I went to help but she seemed okay sitting on the ground. She rested the gun beside her but kept her hand wrapped around the grip.

"Who was that in the car?" I asked. "Because it sure as heck wasn't Eva McLuckie."

"I don't know her name," Eva said. "She's one of the Russian agents. I try to keep her under control, but the drugs required to boost mental resistance are pretty hard to handle."

She was shivering. Not just from the cold.

I looked up at the Hollywood Sign. Then I looked out toward the city. Then I looked back at Eva.

"Give me something to work with."

"The Soviet cell at the Temple of the Magenta Dragon is an advance force. They've been here for years, establishing a foothold by quietly taking over the movie studios."

I nodded as I got the idea. "Starting with Playback Pictures. Rockwell's studio."

"Yes," said Eva. "Chip Rockwell was in deep with a criminal gang—mafia, most likely. The Russians got him out of it but then they owned him. That was all they needed to get started. From there they got contacts at the other studios, and then they could begin seeding their agents across the whole town."

"Seeding?" I didn't like the sound of that much.

"The Soviet advance force is led by a military scientist called Bobrov. He brought over an elite unit headed by a commando called Rokossovsky. They came first to get the transfer operation up and running. Once that was in place, the shipments began."

"Phases one and two, right?"

Eva nodded.

"Keep talking," I said.

"Bobrov has developed a technique that allows him to transfer the mind of one person into the body of another."

I let that sit there for a while on the cold hillside. The Hollywood Sign ran through a few rounds.

Eva said, "You don't believe me, do you?"

"Lady, I'm the last robot in the world. I can believe a lot of things. These shipments, for instance. They wouldn't happen to consist of crystal cubes, about so big?"

I held two hands up and did my best to make a shape with my fingers. Eva looked up and nodded.

"Each cube holds the mind of one agent."

"How many cubes are there?"

"The first shipment was just a few. Bobrov still had work to do to get ready for phase three. It wasn't until he had the full operation running that the rest came in."

"Okay," I said. "So Bobrov and his crew get here first and set up shop. Then the initial seeding was Bobrov replacing the minds of Hollywood film execs with Soviet agents, allowing him to take over the town?"

Eva nodded. "Film executives. Directors and producers. All the top brass. They'd started on actors, too. That's when we were recruited."

"'We'? You and Charles David."

"And others. The Agency got wind of the Soviet infiltration and Bobrov's process, but the studios were already under Soviet control, and that control was spreading, fast. So the agency began recruiting actors to get into Bobrov's inner circle."

"You're telling me you volunteered to get taken over by Soviet agents?"

Eva shook her head. "The Agency developed a drug cocktail to help a subject resist the mind transfer. They work, but only for a time."

"Is this transfer process permanent?"

"It is if you aren't prepared," said Eva. "But the original mind is still there, trapped in the body while the replacement takes it over."

"Charles David had pills. Anti-radiation drugs. The agency gave you those too, right?"

"The transfer process exposes the subject to gamma rays," said Eva. "We needed protection from that, too."

"And the mind cubes themselves are hot."

Then I paused. I found myself scratching my chin. I wondered if Thornton used to do that, too.

"In the basement, you guys all wore protective gear. I assume that was because Chip Rockwell is himself radioactive. I followed a trail out of the Temple and down the street to the theater."

"I'll take your word for that," said Eva. "I don't remember anything once my hitchhiker takes over."

I stepped a little closer. The light from the sign behind me cast my shadow long and deep over the movie star sitting on the ground in front of me. Her expression was set, her lips a perfect level, like she was resigned to the fact that sometimes she wasn't in control of her own body and there wasn't a damn thing she could do about it.

"How do the mind cubes work?"

Eva shrugged.

"Okay," I said. "What about the original Soviet agents? If they get their minds sucked into glass boxes, where does that leave them? Empty shells?"

Eva shrugged for a second time and said, "I don't know."

I paced around a bit.

"What is it?" Eva asked.

I stopped pacing. I looked at Eva. I paced a little more.

"Chip Rockwell is a problem," I said. "His accident three years ago." I tapped my chest. "That accident was me. I had a contract to kill him, so that's what I did. And believe me, I made sure he was dead. Or at least I thought I had, until I saw him in the Temple basement."

Eva pulled herself to her feet and stepped toward me. Her mouth hung open a little, maybe in surprise, or maybe because she was thinking the same thing I was.

I kept talking.

"So what if he *is* still dead. That thing in the basement didn't look much like a person. So what if it isn't?"

"You mean—?"

I nodded. "What if the only thing that survived Chip Rockwell's

death was his *mind*? A mind that now exists inside one of these radioactive cubes."

The sign above us pulsed on as we stood there looking at each
other. I turned and looked up at it.

HOLLY

So I had a handle on Chip Rockwell.

WOOD

Maybe, anyway. It seemed academic for the moment.

HOLLYWOOD

There was something a little more pressing going on.

HOLLYWOOD

Like phase three.

HOLLYWOOD

"Eva," I said. "How many cubes were smuggled into the country
in the phase two shipment?"

"We're not sure, exactly. But it's in the thousands," she said.

"They'll be taking up a lot of space. Where are they being
kept?"

"We're not sure of that either. Presumably a studio backlot. Storage space isn't a problem."

I looked up at the sign. "Phase three. Simultaneous transmission,"
I said. "Nationwide. They're not just beaming *Red Lucky* into movie
theaters, are they? They're beaming Soviet agents into the minds of
the audience, right? Thousands of people, all taken over at once. Possessed by the enemy like *that*."

I snapped my fingers, but all I got was metal sliding silently over
metal.

"Yes," said Eva. "Simultaneous transmission. The perfect inva-
sion."

It was enough to make a robot whistle, if a robot could whistle.
Instead I let a circuit spark and I made a sound more like the
failing brakes of a steam train heard from the next valley over.

Charles David's suggestion that I put a stop to phase three sounded pretty good right about now.

How exactly, I didn't know. I was just about to ask Eva if she had any ideas but it was around then that she yelled something. I couldn't make out what it was, but it sure wasn't English. Then she stumbled backward. She didn't fall over but she nearly did.

The woman looking at me from those dark-ringed eyes wasn't Eva anymore. It was the agent. The *Soviet* agent. Whoever she was.

Then the agent screwed those black eyes shut and she grabbed her bangs with both hands and pulled so hard I thought she was going to scalp herself.

Shouting something that might have been English or Russian or something in between, she spun on her heel and tripped in the dirt. I went to help but she was scrambling away from me already.

"Come on!" yelled Eva.

My Eva.

I followed.

30

We stood behind the Hollywood Sign, lit by the five-phase flashing of the bulbs. They were bright. Really bright. Bright enough that the two seconds between each part of the sequence plunged the whole hillside in darkness as deep as the ocean.

Eva stumbled around. She was fighting it—*her*—and it was a hell of a fight. I wanted to help but all I could do was stick close and grab her in case she took a fall. We were okay where we were but the hill was damn steep and that steepness was very close.

She was muttering under her breath while trying to hold her head onto her shoulders. I kept up. She was looking for something.

"What is it?" I asked. She kept muttering and she kept looking.

I looked up at the back of the sign. There were ladders on the back of the big poles and the whole thing looked so absurdly thin and fragile. It was just a set of thin tin panels set with the lightbulbs, those panels bolted to the back of a frame made of telegraph poles. The whole thing looked like it could have blown over in a breeze that you might not even need to call stiff.

Eva turned and fell onto her backside. She sat there, eyes closed, puffing like she'd run a marathon. I got closer but she waved at me with the hand holding the gun and then she waved the gun at the sign.

I looked back at the sign. I knew two things about it.

One, that it had been refitted for the premiere tomorrow night, practically rebuilt after decades of neglect, the lighting rig alive again after more than forty years of darkness.

Two, that the machine behind the screen at Grauman's Chinese Theatre was connected to the machine on the roof of the same building and that machine was pointed right at the sign.

It didn't take my rusting detective skills to put two and two together. The machines at the theater were part of phase three.

So was the sign.

I looked around. The back of the sign was home to ladders and it was also home to cables. Lots of cables, strapped to the poles with shiny metal cuffs. All those lightbulbs took some juice to light.

And all that juice was powering something else, too. Had to be.

I turned back to Eva. She still had her eyes closed and her chest still went up and down at quite a rate but she looked better. She pointed again without looking.

"The sign. Local-area effect only. Probably wide enough."

She sighed and put her head on her knees. I wished her well in her own battle before I turned back to the sign.

There was my answer. The sign was an amplifier. It was meant for the signal, the one being broadcast from the theater. But local-area effect only? It was wide enough for what? And why only "probably"?

I moved around and stood between the letters and looked down into the valley. From up here you could see nearly all of Los Angeles. Hollywood, certainly, and downtown LA, and a lot more besides. And from down there, with the sign lit like it was, you'd be able to see it for miles and miles.

And miles and miles and miles.

Local-area effect. Probably wide enough.

I looked up at the sign and said something that I was sure Ada wouldn't have approved of.

I turned back to Eva. She was a bundle of nothing lit in a flashing sequence.

"The broadcast isn't just going to movie theaters," I told her, although I had a feeling she already knew what I was about to say. "They're going to flood Los Angeles with the signal, too. Broadcast from here. It's the sign itself—big enough to take in the valley, but not much more."

Eva wasn't talking so I turned back around. I looked at the backs of the panels and at the cables. That's why the sign had been re-electrified. The whole thing was a local-area transmitter.

It seemed phase three—or at least a part of it—was going to be a little easier to solve than I had first thought. Because I was up here alone with Eva and the sign and all I had to do was cut the sign's power. The premiere wasn't until tomorrow but if I could find the power box, maybe the transformer, and do as much damage as possible, that would put the kibosh on this part of the Soviet mind-control plan.

Easy.

Except I wasn't alone with the sign and Eva.

I turned around. Eva was standing up. She had the gun pointed right at me.

Only it wasn't Eva, not anymore. It was someone else driving Eva's body around while Eva's own mind swam around in the pool, looking for the ladder out.

The Russian agent barked an instruction I didn't understand but got the drift of. I stepped away from the sign as she stepped closer to it. I didn't know what that gun was but I didn't want to test it out.

While we danced I scanned the sign. I was looking for junction boxes, fuse boxes, anything I could tear out with my bare steel hands.

That was why my Eva had brought me up here, after all. She needed me and those hands to do what she couldn't and sabotage the sign. With the local-area transmitter disabled we could then focus on the works at the theater.

"Hey, Eva, you in there?" I asked.

The Russian agent crinkled her nose. I didn't like the expression. Eva wouldn't have pulled it. It made me sick to my stomach to think there was someone else in charge.

If I had a stomach, of course.

Then the agent wearing a movie star's body rocked on her heels. She closed her eyes. The gun went down.

I saw opportunity knocking so I opened the door. Diving fast, I almost got it, too, but the agent was faster.

The Russian agent looked out at me with a firm hold on her piece. She screamed and then I saw it in her eyes: Eva was back. Back and fighting but not winning that fight.

"The top!" she yelled. "There's a master control box. Come on!"

She turned and headed for the ladder nearest and began climbing up the giant letter *O* that stood next to the giant letter *H*. She climbed fast. By the time I hit the bottom rung she was nearly halfway up and then soon enough she disappeared from view as she reached the summit ahead of me. I kept climbing.

I stopped once I was at the top. I could hardly go any farther because there was nothing for me to stand on, just a narrow wooden pole that formed the top of the letter.

Farther along that letter, Eva crawled on her hands and knees. She was making good time toward a big box I could see at the other end of the letter. I had to figure out a way of helping her but crawling along the sign didn't look like much of an option for a robot of my proportions. I looked back down the ladder. Maybe I was better off killing cables at ground level.

"Eva! I'll go back down and see what I can do—"

Eva stopped crawling and managed to rotate herself around without falling off the sign. She got herself up onto her haunches. She looked at me. Then she closed her eyes and she rubbed her forehead. There was pain there. Real, physical pain. Her fight with the Soviet agent trying to wrestle permanent control of her body had pushed her to her very limits.

I didn't like the way she looked. The breeze picked up and she swayed in it. She looked out across a view that was to die for. The wind gusted and her body moved with it. Anything more and this movie star was going to have just the wrong kind of Hollywood ending.

I had to get her back to safety so we could smash something up at a safer altitude.

"Okay, just hold on," I said, all the while calculating the possibilities. The top of the letter O was narrow, but maybe if I crawled like her I could get across. I adjusted my footing on the ladder and got ready to move.

Then she snapped out of it and she nodded and turned back to me. She returned to her hands and knees and took a slow and careful movement toward me.

I waved her an encouragement. "That's it, back you come. Easy does it."

Eva stopped crawling and curled her head into her chest. Then she looked up at me and she snarled, her nose and forehead creasing in anger. The Soviet agent was back in charge. She yelled something at me and then she fumbled with something in the pocket of her dress.

She lifted out Special Agent Touch Daley's special gun.

I assume she fired it too, but I don't remember that part. What I do remember is a flash of light that seemed brighter than the blaze of the lights of the sign and when I tried to move I found there was nothing for me to move against—no ground, no ladder, no sign. Nothing but thin, thin air.

Then I saw shapes that looked like giant letters spelling out the name of a famous place as they flashed in a sequence of bright light.

HOLLY

The word seemed to get smaller and smaller

 WOOD

 and it was then I realized I was falling

  HOLLYWOOD

  and quite a long way too

   HOLLYWOOD

   and I had a feeling this was going to hurt

    HOLLYWOOD

    and probably hurt quite a lot.

31

I opened my eyes. It was dark but the darkness was moving, like it was raining at night. A real hurricane, the kind that blew palm trees clean out of the ground when the wind made landfall on small islands. The rain was sideways, which made sense given the wind, which roared like a jet engine in my ears. There was light from somewhere because the raindrops were glittering in red and blue.

There was a flash of lightning. I tried to move and found I couldn't. I was lying on something and I was strapped down. Something must have been up with my gyroscope because it felt like I was, if not entirely upright, then leaning back only by degrees.

The lightning flashed again and then the rain seemed to change direction and color. There was a click in my audio receptors, loud enough to be heard over the storm, and then the storm was gone as that part of my sensory input array reset itself.

I checked the time. I checked it twice and I still didn't believe it. It was Friday night.

Except it couldn't be. I checked again. It was. Maybe my chronometer had taken a knock because if it was Friday, that meant I'd been awake for a long time. Too long. Beyond my battery life. Beyond the length of the memory tape in my chest.

Both impossible.

Maybe I was deactivated and dreaming in my electric sleep.

What I heard next was the sound of a crowd in a large room with great acoustics. It was a steady mumble, soft and not unpleasant to listen to.

Then the lightning flashed again as my optics came back online.

I opened my eyes and I looked around and I said, "This is quite the welcoming committee."

They were standing in a semicircle in front of me and I figured out what my gyroscope had been trying to tell me. I was strapped to something made of three separate pieces, padded but only thinly. My feet were sitting on a rest. There was a big leather band around my legs, and each arm was likewise attached to an armrest.

A super-duper dentist's chair, like the one in the honeymoon suite of the Ritz-Beverly Hotel. It was folded out and tilted up so I was nearly but not quite standing.

From my left to my right stood the A-listers, the big guns of Hollywood, the rich and the famous. The crowd was three deep and while all of them were done up to the nines, they were all also wearing the big, heavy, protective glasses. The black smocks were absent.

The first row was full of stars I recognized. Alaska Gray with her long white hair blending into the silver furs draped around her shoulders. The one and only Rico Spillane and his two friends, Parker Silverwood and Bob Thatcher. Behind them were others I didn't know but I had a feeling were probably on display at the ice cream parlor. Only Charles David didn't seem to be there, on account of him being dead.

But I did know the two celebrities standing front and center. One in a long red dress, her black hair bigger than ever, the eyes behind the dark glasses I knew to be circled with thick makeup like two black shotgun barrels. Next to her, a man with a stiff wave in his hair and a jacket you could see from space and it still wouldn't be far enough away. He was smiling so much it pushed the big glasses up his face.

Eva wasn't holding the gun anymore. It had packed quite a punch, although I guessed the fall off the Hollywood Sign hadn't done me much good either.

Fresco Peterman fiddled with a cuff link and he was looking at me with his head tilted in a way that told me he was acting out the grand finale of his latest picture. Once an actor, always an actor.

I ignored him. I looked at Eva. She didn't speak either, which was a shame, because I wanted to hear if she had a Russian accent or not. Her expression was hard but it was difficult to tell if it was her or not. If I'd ever really been able to tell anyway.

I pulled on the straps holding me to the chair but it was no use, which was a surprise given a leather strap, even a fat one with a big buckle, shouldn't have been much of a problem. So I pulled again and was rewarded with an alarm ringing somewhere inside my head that told me to sit still while my system ran through an emergency diagnostic. For my own safety, said the alert, my primary motor units were disengaged. I couldn't have moved even if I had wanted to, which was really quite a lot.

Something else had happened to me, something after being shot with the weird gun and falling down a mountain. Something unexpected.

Because when I queried the emergency diagnostic I was told that my battery was at 100 percent charge. And when I queried the reading again and asked for voltage and capacity, I got back numbers that were different from what they should have been.

I was at running at full power from batteries with twice the capacity as before.

New batteries.

Someone had been busy.

I looked around. The room was big, the ceiling too high. It was all black and lit with fluorescent strips that seemed to be straining. The rumble of the audience was somewhere behind me.

Grauman's Chinese Theatre. I was backstage, behind the cinema screen itself. The premiere was due to start in—

Thirty minutes.

Oh boy.

My diagnostic continued to fly and there was no way I could override it. All I could do was sit tight. At least I was still awake. Awake and thinking and—

And I could remember yesterday. I remembered it all. Where I went. Who I spoke to and what I said.

The ride up the hill. Eva McLuckie fighting the parasite inside her mind.

The fall off the letter *O*.

My batteries weren't the only thing that had been replaced.

Ada. I had to talk to Ada. She would be looking for me. I had a built-in tracker and I hadn't got back to the office, so she would be looking for me. She would have organized something. A search party. She had contacts. Plenty of them. Hell, she could just call the authorities. Thornton might have been long dead but there must have been some part of the government still keeping an eye on us, even if Ada had to hide what we were up to. Someone had to keep her maintained. Me, too.

I thought for a moment about Special Agent Touch Daley and his classified department. I thought it would have been really good for him to come bursting into the theater with a whole lot of other agents, special or otherwise.

Any.

Minute.

Now.

The A-list row was still watching me. Touch Daley had failed to burst in anywhere. I had another look through the transcript the emergency diagnostic was spewing onto my new memory tape and saw my tracker had been disabled. Deliberately, of course.

Someone really had been busy. Someone who knew exactly what they were doing.

Fresco took a step closer to me and leaned in over my semi-reclined face. He finished fiddling with his cuff link and leaned on the side of my chair.

"There's someone here who has been looking forward to seeing you for a long time, Sparks," he said in heavily accented English. He smiled and his Hollywood teeth shone.

The semicircle of A-listers parted straight down the middle. Through that middle came a trio made up of two men walking and a third in a wheelchair. The man doing the pushing was young and strong and his hair was short. Military short. He was not only wearing a black smock fastened high at the neck, but he had on the big protective glasses and the big protective gloves, too. The gloves went up nearly to his elbow.

Artem Rokossovsky. I remembered him.

The other man was older, smaller, thinner, sunken cheeks and a pointed chin and a gray pompadour that looked too big for his head. He was the only person not wearing protective glasses, but he was dressed in the black smock like his pal. He wasn't smiling but his expression told me everything I needed to know about how he thought the night was going and in whose favor.

Vitaly Bobrov himself. Robot scientist, Russian military. The brains behind the Hollywood Reds.

I also knew who the man in the wheelchair was. His lower half was covered with a thick woolen blanket in equally thick plaid. His upper half was wearing a dinner jacket and bow tie, like he'd gone to the effort to dress up for the occasion even if Bobrov and his assistant hadn't. Above the dinner jacket was a head wrapped in bandages with a pair of dark glasses stuck onto the front.

"RAYMOND ELECTROMATIC," said Chip Rockwell with a voice that sounded like someone kicking over a beehive. "I HAVE BEEN JUST DYING TO SEE YOU AGAIN."

I didn't speak. I just looked.

Then Rockwell spoke again.

"DR. BOBROV, PREPARE OUR GUEST FOR PHASE FOUR."

Bobrov's thin and old face cracked open and he laughed, and he laughed for a long, long time.

32

Fresco Peterman and his pal Rico Spillane spun me around and I found myself facing another of the chairs, this one set up on the other side of the big machine with the silver disk that sat behind the cinema screen. The other chair was, like mine, folded flat and tilted upright. The chair was empty. I wondered who was going to be strapped into it for phase four.

Whatever phase four was.

There was more gear here than before. Some consoles on wheels and panels with lights and buttons that wouldn't have looked out of place back in Ada's computer room. The other chair was hooked up to it and the folk who had wheeled me in ducked down behind my chair and began hooking it up too while Artem wheeled Rockwell around to a spot between the two chairs. Bobrov meanwhile had got over his fit of hilarity and walked over to the empty chair. He swung the jointed arm with the miniature disk and claw device on the end of it around so it was above the headrest.

With everyone apparently minding their own business I ran through my diagnostic log again. There were reports and feedback from circuits and systems I didn't recognize. I had no idea what the hell had been done to me during my missing day, but I didn't count on it being good.

And yet, here I was. Alive and kicking but for the fact that the former was never going to be true and the latter was not a currently available option.

But while I couldn't kick I could move my head a little, so I lifted it and looked down at my chest, where I knew my magnetic memory tape was supposed to be spinning away—but which the diagnostic log told me was missing. I saw that wasn't the only thing missing.

I wasn't wearing my shirt or jacket. My chest hatch was gone too, leaving my innards exposed. I couldn't see too well from this angle, but I could see enough.

Where my tape would sit was something else. It was glassy and glowed a faint pink. All I could see was the upper edge, but it was enough.

There was a buzzing sound mixed with the sound of a detuned radio. I looked up after I realized that the noise was Rockwell laughing.

"What have you done to me?" I asked. I had a pretty good idea I knew the answer.

"YOU HAVE BEEN UPGRADED."

That's why I'd been out for more than a full day. After my fall from the sign they'd picked me up and switched me off.

And installed one of their magic cubes, replacing my memory tape.

"AN INFINITELY LARGE MEMORY STORE," said Rockwell in his buzz-saw monotone. "A DIGITAL CRYSTAL EMBEDDED WITH A BINARY MATRIX IN THREE DIMENSIONS AND DECODED BY A LASER BEAM READER."

"You're pretty smart for a movie producer," I said. "Taken a night class?"

Rockwell laughed again and this time Bobrov joined him as he made adjustments to the other chair.

"Your creator, Professor Thornton, was a very talented man, my friend," Bobrov said in an accent thick enough to hang wallpaper on. "Do you know we tried to make him turn, several times. Each time he refused. Such misguided loyalty from one so great. Fortunately for us, those in his laboratory were not so, how shall we say, *committed* to this failed experiment you call a country."

While he spoke, Bobrov's old army buddy Artem stood next to his boss with his big arms folded and his mouth firmly shut. I wondered if he spoke English.

"So the magic crystals are from Thornton," I said. This made me feel a little better—not much, but I was happy to take what I was given. Maybe if I hadn't killed Thornton I would have got an upgrade at some point.

Shame.

"Funny," I said, "I thought you were a robot scientist yourself. Why did you need to go stealing someone else's work?"

Bobrov had finished his setup and made a show of wiping his hands very slowly on his long black smock. He turned to face me.

"A wise man once said," he replied, "that talent borrows and genius *steals*."

Bobrov seemed pretty pleased with that line because he did some more of his old-man cackle. I ran his words around a few times but they still sounded fishy to me.

I nodded at the empty chair. "You know, I saw a chair like that at the Ritz-Beverly? I didn't think it matched the curtains very well."

Bobrov shrugged like he couldn't have cared less, and I'm pretty sure he couldn't have.

"Did you know," I said, "that there was a break-in at Thornton's lab? I have a feeling you're not the only one with an eye on his gear."

At this, Bobrov said something to Artem in Russian and Artem nodded and moved out of my field of vision. Then Bobrov returned his attention to the empty chair and made some more adjustments before turning back and clapping his hands. He looked as pleased as punch. I guess I didn't blame him. His plan seemed to be running pretty smoothly, after all.

I wondered about Rockwell. He hadn't said much. I wondered what was left of him underneath the bandages.

Bobrov clapped his hands again and moved to address the bunch of actors I knew were still standing behind me.

"Take your places, Comrades. The moment is near. Soon phase three will be initiated and the program can move to the next phase. You have your instructions."

The A-listers didn't say anything in return, but I could hear them leave and I could imagine them all slipping their protective goggles off, tucking them into tuxedos and slipping them down dress fronts. Time was ticking down to the premiere and they were all needed out front. Even the Soviet agents didn't want to disappoint their public. Maybe they were getting a taste for it.

As they all left, one tapped me on the shoulder.

"Good luck, Sparks," said Fresco, right into my audio receptor, and then he joined the others.

I looked at Rockwell. "So you going to tell me about phase four, then?"

Rockwell was completely still. When he spoke I had to admit, it was eerie, the way that voice came out from what was otherwise a completely inanimate object.

"YOU WILL NEED TO DO BETTER THAN THAT," he said.

"Oh, okay," I said. "So what else can we talk about? Defected to any good enemy states recently? Oh, say, how about you tell me about how I killed you three years ago and then you came back to life as a mummy. I love a good horror story."

And then Rockwell performed his next trick, one that took me and Bobrov both by surprise.

He stood up.

"What are you doing?" asked Bobrov. He reached for Rockwell but Rockwell knocked his hands away. Rockwell pushed himself up out of the wheelchair with hands that were simple metal clamps. He stood and the blanket dropped to the floor.

His lower half was mechanical, just a simple set of levered and jointed struts that served as legs and two rectangular plates with a hinge in the middle that served as feet. Rockwell's shirttails hung down nearly to his knees, like he was a well-dressed country gent who had been caught by the butler doing something he shouldn't have been.

Rockwell took one step toward me. Then another. It was slow, the walk of someone learning to walk again after a bad road traffic accident. Bobrov hovered nearby with a frown on his face and his arms held out behind Rockwell like he was a shepherd repositioning his flock.

"OH, YOU KILLED ME," said Rockwell. "MAKE NO MISTAKE, ROBOT. CHIP ROCKWELL DIED THAT NIGHT THREE YEARS AGO."

"Well you're doing pretty well for a dead guy, Comrade," I said. "All things considered, anyway."

"MY CONDITION IS A TEMPORARY ONE," said Rockwell. "I WAS FORTUNATE TO BE PART OF A GREAT PLAN AT THE TIME OF MY MUR-DER. AN EXPERIMENT DESTINED TO CHANGE THE COURSE OF HUMAN HISTORY."

"I like a dead guy with ambition," I said. "Don't tell me—your Russian buddies found you just in time and had you copied off onto a magic cube before you died."

Rockwell swung another step toward me. Bobrov backed away and checked his watch. He looked up at the big machine towering above us all and then he went to one of the consoles. He hissed between gritted teeth. Rockwell's little performance was clearly unexpected.

"I WAS THE FIRST," said Rockwell. "THE TRANSFER PROCESS WAS EXPERIMENTAL AND NEEDED TESTING. THAT TEST PROVED TO BE A RESOUNDING SUCCESS."

"Pardon me for saying," I said, "but you don't look much like a resounding success. But sure, experimental, huh? Is that why they kept you around? Because it seems to me that your Russian buddies have a good grip on your studio and would be able to run it pretty well without you. You're a test subject. Because otherwise you'd be walking around in someone else's body instead of this contraption, right? Something tells me Bobrov's experiment is still going. But look, if you plan on ruling the world with your friend here it seems you'd want to be more mobile."

"AS I SAID, A TEMPORARY SITUATION WE ARE ABOUT TO RECTIFY."

Rockwell swung around on the edge of one of his flat metal feet and nearly fell backward as he did so. But he kept his balance and pointed with one claw at the empty chair opposite.

"PHASE FOUR IS ABOUT TO START," he said.

I looked at the chair. I looked at Rockwell. I looked down and saw the pinkish glow of the digital crystal installed in my chest.

Phase four.

Now I finally got it. Chip Rockwell didn't want to make his new home in just anybody.

He wanted *me*.

Just like Charles David had said, only I hadn't understood what he meant.

Rockwell buzzed quietly to himself. He was laughing again, or maybe his temporary shell of a body was shorting out after all that exertion.

"Okay, very nice," I said. "Your mind, my body. Neat. But why here? Why now? Haven't you got enough on your plate with phase three without trying to fit in a little mind-swapping at the same time?"

"Power," said Bobrov. He continued to work but he at least nodded at the machine that stood above us all. "Transferring a mind into an artificial system like you requires a greater energy flow. The transmission system can provide that power without compromising its own function."

"Huh," I said. "Well, fancy that."

Rockwell swung back around to me. For a moment I thought he was going to keep going and fall right onto me, but he stopped in time and wobbled for a few seconds. He was close, his dark glasses practically touching my face. Now I could see what was on the other side of them, and it was nothing, just more of the cream bandages wound tight as you like.

"IT IS MAGNIFICENT, MAGNIFICENT," he said and I knew he was talking about me. "THORNTON WAS A GENIUS. A SHAME HE COULD NOT BE TURNED, DR. BOBROV. HIS WORKMANSHIP BORDERS THE DIVINE. UNLIKE YOURS."

Bobrov didn't look up from his console. "Yours was a temporary solution, Rockwell. You know that. I had neither the facilities nor the equipment to build you a better form. The program took priority."

Rockwell managed something close to a nod, the bandages covering his head rubbing against my face.

"DON'T WORRY, DR. BOBROV, I WON'T HOLD THAT AGAINST YOU. THIS TEMPORARY SOLUTION IS ABOUT TO BECOME PERMANENT."

He turned to the Soviet scientist and pointed with a claw.

Bobrov nodded and bent down to slide a case out from next to one of the consoles. The case was big and square and had a heavy lid with a catch that he flicked. With the lid swung back he reached in and took out one of the digital crystals. He looked at the thing, smirked to himself, then went back to the empty chair and slid the cube into the claw that hung on the articulated arm. Then he wiped his hands off and walked back to the console while watching his watch and moving a finger in the air like he was counting a beat.

Then he gestured with both hands to the big machine behind the screen.

"Phase three begins."

He threw a lever with a dramatic flourish I really couldn't blame him for, and the disk mounted on the front of the machine began to spin. It picked up speed and began to whine loud enough to be heard out in the auditorium. Bobrov took a step back and wiped his hands with what looked like unnecessary vigor as he admired the workings of the machine in front of him.

There was a blast of music, a brassy fanfare followed by tumbling violins and a roll of thunder from the kettledrums. The screen was lit in bright silver and shadows moved across it.

The premiere of *Red Lucky*—aka phase three—had started.

Rockwell looked up at the moving shapes, and as the orchestra swelled he turned back to me.

"AT LAST, TIME FOR PHASE FOUR."

That was when Artem Rokossovsky stepped up behind Rockwell and slammed a heavy wrench into the back of Rockwell's bandaged head.

33

Rockwell went over cleanly while wailing like a detuned radio. He crashed to the ground next to my chair and lay there twitching and sparking and buzzing like a wasp trapped under a glass.

Artem looked down at this piece of handiwork. He smiled a smile of intense professional satisfaction then he looked at the wrench in his hand like he didn't know what it was before dropping it onto Rockwell's body.

The music was still playing, as loud as you like. The shapes on the screen moved and people began to speak. Their voices were deep and booming. So close to the front-of-house speakers it was liable to give you a headache.

"*Now* we can begin," said Bobrov. He laughed and his laugh was caught in the swell of the music and was carried away by it. He moved around to the other chair and stepped up into the footrests, then lay back. He reached up and positioned the disk and the claw with the cube in it over his face.

The consoles winked. Their lights wouldn't be seen from the auditorium proper. The audience sitting just yards away would have no idea what was going on behind the scenes as they watched the mammoth movie screen.

I looked down as best I could. Rockwell was rocking on the floor but he couldn't get up. I don't know if he was trying to speak but all that came from him was something that sounded dangerous and electric.

"You were very useful, Comrade," said Bobrov as he got himself comfortable. "But as you said yourself, this was a temporary arrangement."

It took me a moment to realize he was talking to Rockwell, not me. Bobrov lay back in his chair.

The digital crystal hanging over his head was glowing pink now and I couldn't see his face beyond it.

"Something tells me Rockwell wasn't quite in the picture," I said.

"Rockwell and his studio were necessary for a time," said Bobrov. "His studio already had a system in place for money laundering that was perfectly suited to our needs. And with his untimely demise he provided us the final proof that the transfer process was possible. Stepping-stones, Mr. Electromatic, stepping-stones."

I tuned into my Geiger counter and turned it up. It crackled like bacon in a pan. As Eva had said, the whole process resulted in significant radiation exposure. Not enough to be fatal so long as you took precautions, but I wondered how far a daily diet of potassium iodide tablets would stretch.

Particularly for someone who had been working on the equipment and the technique for a long time. For years, in fact.

Like Bobrov.

Bobrov was old and frail but there was something else I'd noticed when I first laid my optics on him. The vampire pallor, the thinness to his cheeks.

He was on the way out, but he thought he'd found a solution.

"You think you'll be able to live in a chassis like mine, huh?" I called out over what seemed to be a Western gunfight taking place on the other side of the screen. I thanked the composer of the musical score for his overindulgence, otherwise the auditorium would be listening in on our conversation. "I get it, Comrade. Radiation sickness. Too much exposure over too long a time."

I could see Bobrov shake his head but that was about all I could see.

"Cancer," said Bobrov. He laughed. "Tell me, robot man. We can build machines that can land on the moon. We can build machines that can walk and talk and think like men. We can build a machine that allows one mind to be transferred into another. We truly live in an age of miracles."

"I sense there's a *but* coming."

"But," said Bobrov, and I had a feeling he hadn't heard me, "there are still some problems we face that cannot be solved. The cancer I have is incurable, inoperable. My own body has failed me. And yet here I am, about to make a great transcendence. I shall become immortal, and I shall lead the program for the next thousand years."

I felt like pointing out the difference between eternity and a very long time but this didn't seem to be the moment. The disk hanging over my chair didn't have a cube in the claw behind it because that cube was in my chest, and I had an inkling that any moment now my mind was about to be pushed out by the mind of the man seated opposite.

The disk spun on the machine above us. It spun pretty fast. The whine was picking up, too, turning into a tornadic howl that someone was going to notice.

There was a thud from somewhere next to me, and then I caught movement out of the corner of my eye. It looked vaguely like a tree falling.

I glanced sideways and saw Artem hit the deck, his eyes closed and his expression less surprised than a little disappointed.

There was a tugging on my arm. I turned my head and saw wavy hair that looked wet. Then Fresco Peterman looked up at me from behind his dark glasses.

"Quick, Sparks, time to go." There was no doubting his accent now. He could have sung "The Star-Spangled Banner" at the opening of the World Series with a voice like that.

I looked down. He was working at the strap holding my left wrist to the armrest. I glanced at Bobrov but the glow from his crystal was pretty big and I wasn't sure he could see us. I don't even think he'd seen his old army buddy go down.

My hand came free. Fresco reached around to the other one and released the buckle and then he stood back and looked at me. After a couple of seconds he gave me the hurry-up by waving his hands.

I tried to move but the emergency override was still in place. I had a poke around in the log to see if I could override the override, but it was going to take a little bit of time. I told Fresco the same and then I said, "Forget me. Evacuate the auditorium, quick smart."

Fresco shook his head and his hair didn't move an inch. "Already taken care of. Eva has everyone outside. The other theaters are clearing out, too."

"Eva?"

Fresco patted my shoulder. "She's fine, Sparks. Don't worry about it."

Then he looked up at the machine with the spinning disk. I followed his gaze.

"But we're still transmitting?" I asked.

Fresco nodded. Then he grabbed for something inside the thing he was wearing that he thought was a dinner jacket. He pulled out Agent Daley's strange gun and he aimed it at the machine.

Bobrov was on him in an instant. His exit from his chair had been hidden behind the pink glow but the way the old man roared when he tackled Fresco suggested he was none too pleased with his interference. The two of them went down and began wrestling on the floor. Fresco was a big guy and had managed to surprise Artem with a knockout punch, but his footballer physique was matched for now by the weaker Bobrov's sheer desperation.

Then an alert rang around my head like a church bell and I was a robot in control of his own body again. I stood from the chair and I went to help Fresco but just as I moved something grabbed me around the wrist with a grip like a damn vise. Then I was pulled around with more than a little violence.

Bobrov wasn't the only one who had found a hidden strength.

Rockwell stood before me, one of his clamp hands holding me tight. He pulled my wrist down and I had no choice but to go with it. Sure enough I was on my knees in two seconds flat.

I looked up at his face. The bandages were unraveling and tangled around his metal frame legs. The glasses were still there. I had a feeling I didn't want to see what the bandages hid.

Then I saw something else. He had a power lead, a fat one with a corrugated rubbery surface, jammed down the front of his shirt. The lead ran to the console behind him. I could see dials on that console and all of them were redlining.

It seemed he was going to take a little of that extra energy flow for himself.

Rockwell stared at me with those dark glasses and his voice buzzed at me like saw blades going through lumber. If he was shouting real words or just screaming in rage, it all sounded the same to me.

I screamed in rage myself. I pushed myself up. Rockwell was strong but he was still a fragile thing that lacked poise and balance. I was big and bulky, solid as anything and twice as heavy. I pushed up with my legs and out with my arms and something broke in Rockwell's arm. It levered upward and he staggered backward.

I turned and went for Bobrov and Fresco. The gun was still in Fresco's hand but keeping a hold of it was impeding his fight.

Two clamps around my neck this time. I grabbed at them and tried to pry them off. I was working hard at it but they had good leverage. Rockwell got his face against my ear and buzzed and buzzed and buzzed.

There was a bang and a flash and the clamps were gone. I fell forward against my chair. I spun and got back to my feet.

Eva McLuckie was standing there in her red dress and those dark glasses, holding the thick black cable that used to be plugged into Rockwell sparking in one hand. Rockwell shuddered on his feet in front of her. I wasted no time, sending a punch toward his glasses with enough force to stop a bus. As soon as it connected his buzzing stopped and he flew backward, landing against the machine. Eva cried out in surprise and I grabbed her, throwing myself around so I was between her and Rockwell.

There was a distant explosion. Whatever Rockwell had broken with his fall, the big machine was spinning out of control. It rocked in the frame, enough to shake the theater to its foundations and send dust and debris raining down on us. With Eva in front of me I hunched around her for protection and pushed the pair of us forward toward Fresco. He got free of Bobrov and scooted toward me, wrapping his body around Eva from the other side.

I looked up. Bobrov rolled to his feet. He had blood on his face and his smock was torn. He looked at me. Then he noticed Artem unconscious on the floor and he started yelling something in Russian.

There was another bang from behind us and I saw the lick of flame reflected in Bobrov's eyes before I saw the fire itself.

I put my head down and pulled Fresco and Eva in tight, hoping it'd be enough.

Then there was a lot of light, and a lot of heat.

Another bang.

I was pretty sure that this time, it was me.

34

I was upright. So far, so good. I felt cold. That was a little alarming in that I knew I couldn't feel cold. Or hot, for that matter.

Actually, that wasn't true. I could feel hot and cold. I could sense them and measure them. But they didn't bother me, not usually. My operating range was pretty wide.

But the fact was I was cold. Cold and tired. I had circuits shorting all the way down one side and my logic gates were flipping like a casino croupier shuffling the decks.

And I hurt. A lot. This, too, was nonsense. A scientific impossibility. Didn't stop it from being the truth, though. Of course it wasn't real pain. I figured out that much. It was an echo, a template of pain taken from the template of a man.

The template of Professor Thornton, my creator.

I heard the ticking of the second hand of a fast watch. I smelled cigarettes and bad coffee and the smell of pine-scented furniture polish filling a hot and stuffy office.

I closed my eyes. I opened them. Made no difference. My optics weren't working. Or maybe they were, but all I could see was the flashing afterimage of a woman with big hair dressed in tight slacks and a tighter sweater holding a steaming mug in one hand and a cigarette between the first two fingers of the other hand. The cigarette was held up in the air like she had to an important message to tell the world. Her hair was blond and her makeup was too thick but I liked her smile.

She pointed at something and then she was gone, dust on the wind, a dream half-forgotten.

There were people near. Specifically, two people.

"Like this?" said the first. A man's voice. Familiar, but I couldn't place it. A good, strong voice. The kind of voice that could sell you soap on the TV and you'd like it.

"Careful!" A woman. Young. Young but confident.

"No, honey, you're doing it wrong. Look, try again, only this time . . ."

Three people, not two. This one was a woman, too. Older. Her voice deeper, the result of a twenty-a-day habit.

Ada.

I felt a tugging sensation. I felt hands on me. Four hands, rocking my chassis, trying to get something plugged into my front.

"He's leaking," said the man. "Oh, dammit, my jacket!"

"It'll come out," said Ada. "I'll give you the name of my dry cleaner. Just down the street. They're good, too. Maybe you can slip them some extra and they'll lose it for you."

"Almost got it," said the young woman.

"Steady," said the man. "And what's wrong with my jacket? I like my jacket!"

"I can recommend a therapist, too," said Ada.

I checked my clock. It was late. Too late.

And it didn't bother me. I could remember.

"Ready?" asked Ada.

I could remember everything.

"Hey," said the man. Maybe I'd moved. It was a little hard to tell. "Just hold on, Sparks, one thing at a time."

"Here goes nothing," said Ada.

And then my alarm went off and I woke up to another beautiful morning in Los Angeles.

35

They stood in front of me, the pair of them, he in a houndstooth jacket that looked like a TV screen tuned to thin air and her in a black dress. The big black rings of makeup were gone from around her eyes. I thought she looked better this way.

Fresco must have seen I was awake. He didn't move any except to crack his famous smile. "Hey, Sparks, welcome back to the land of the living."

I smiled on the inside and I looked at the ceiling while I tried to figure out what was what. We were in the computer room back at the office.

"What happened to our privacy policy, Ada? I really don't want to have to kill these two."

There was a sound like someone taking a long, long drag on a cigarette, then a sort of dull popping sound like someone blowing out a lungful of hot smoke.

"The exception proves the rule, Chief," said Ada.

"I'm not sure that means what you think it means."

"They're fine. I cleared them."

"Oh," I said.

I looked down. I was in my alcove. I was missing my suit. I was also missing my detective's shield, which should have been on my chest. In its place was a metal plate a different color from the rest of me. It bulged a little more, making my front rounded instead of flat.

I tapped at it with a finger.

Fresco's smile dropped and he looked sideways at Eva and she looked back at him. For the first time I noticed they were holding hands.

Then Fresco turned back to me, seemed to hold his breath, and he tapped his cheek with a finger.

I reached up to my own face and felt it. There was a scratch under one eye. Not very deep, not very long, but a scratch all the same.

Seems there was something that could ding the special bronzed steel alloy that Thornton and Thornton's bosses had been so pleased with.

Something like a building falling on top of me, for instance.

Fresco looked like he was about to cry. Then Ada laughed.

"Relax, Peterman, Ray's just being a big baby. Aren't you going to say thanks, Ray?"

I looked at the ceiling. "I was getting to it."

"Uh-huh."

"Would help if I knew what I was saying thanks for, of course."

Fresco didn't move. Eva sighed and let go of his hand and reached for the newspaper on the table behind them and handed it over to me.

I turned it over and unfolded it so I was back at the start. The headline caught my eye. It was hard to miss.

FIRE AT NATIONWIDE PREMIERE
GRAUMAN'S CHINESE THEATRE SEVERELY DAMAGED
EXPERIMENTAL BROADCAST SYSTEM BLAMED

I read the article. There had been a fire at the theater. It had started a few minutes into the premiere of *Red Lucky*, forcing the cancellation of the nationwide simultaneous transmission, but fortunately everyone had got out thanks to the efforts of one of the movie's own stars, one Eva McLuckie, who had reappeared on the red carpet after months away from the public eye to the rapturous adoration of the assembled press and gathered fans alike.

I lowered the paper and looked at Fresco.

"A fire, huh?"

Fresco's smile returned. "Hey, you saved us back there, big fella. The whole damn roof came down, crash!" He mimed the roof coming down, with both hands no less. "If it weren't for you, we'd be flattened."

That explained a few things.

"What about the transmitter?"

"Destroyed in the fire," said Eva. "We have a cleanup crew at the theater sifting through the wreckage."

"They're up at the sign, too," said Fresco. "They're dismantling the amplifier."

I nodded. The two of them stood in front of me with expectant expressions. Like I was in charge of something.

"Rockwell and Bobrov?" I asked.

"Rockwell's body was recovered at the theater," said Eva. "There's not much left of him."

"And Bobrov?"

Fresco answered. "Missing at the moment, but we're pretty sure he was caught in the roof collapse. His assistant, too—Rokossovsky. We were right in the middle of it."

"What about the Soviet cell? You weren't all CIA agents, were you?"

"No," said Fresco. "But they're being taken care of. The Agency has cooked up a way to de-process anyone who went through the Soviet mind transfer. They'll all be back to normal soon enough."

I smiled on the inside. "That's a lot of cases of nervous exhaustion."

"The *Daily News* is going to have a field day," said Fresco. He frowned. "Vampires, the lot of them."

"And how about you two?"

"We've had one round already," said Eva. "One more and we'll be cleared."

Fresco nodded. "But we're still going to be taking a lot of pills for a while."

"Seems a small price," I said. "What about Bobrov's gang? The crew he brought over with him from the Motherland?"

"The rest of Bobrov's unit was rounded up at Charles David's house," said Eva. "We're still searching studio backlots for the Soviet shipments."

I nodded. For a moment I had a vision of a car park on a rainy night and a big building and someone walking into it, his head hunkered down against the rain.

And then the vision was gone.

I blinked, or I thought I did, and the two movie stars were staring at me.

"The hotel," I said. "What were you and Charles David doing with all that gear in the honeymoon suite? Bobrov didn't seem to know anything about that."

"Nothing to do with me, Sparks," he said and he opened his arms and gave a little bow to Eva. "My team was me and Alaska."

"Alaska Gray?"

"One and the same," he said, and then he dropped his arms. "She's fine, don't worry. Little smoke inhalation."

I looked at Eva. "And the hotel?"

Eva twisted her fingers in front of her. "We learned that Bobrov's mental transfer process was based on something stolen from Professor Thornton's lab. There had been some leaks in the months before Thornton's death—the Soviets had managed to buy some of Thornton's scientists, we think. Anyway, we knew that Thornton's facility was sealed, but if we could get some of his equipment out and find out how it worked, we thought we could find out how to reverse the transfer process. Charles wasn't handling the drugs the CIA had given us very well. He arranged to get the equipment out and to the hotel. Seemed as good a place as any—the Ritz-Beverly prides itself on discretion for people in our line of work."

So Charles David had been responsible for the lab break-in—the one that had sent Special Agent Touch Daley after me.

I still needed to have a talk to Ada about that.

"But the hotel is being cleared out and decontaminated," said Eva.

"Well, that's good," I said. I pulled myself out of my alcove. They made room for me as I went to the window and looked out of it. The sun was rising and the building opposite was no prettier than it had been every other morning I looked at it.

"Figuring out Thornton's equipment sounds like a bit of a tall order for two movie actors," I said, turning back to Eva. "If you don't mind me saying."

Fresco laughed at this. I looked at him and he kept laughing and then I looked at Eva.

"Mr. Peterman here," she said, "was a physicist before he took up acting. Charles David left college to work as a mathematician for the DORL. I have a degree in computational complexity theory and was working at MIT before I decided to hang it all and get some of that LA sunshine I'd read about in *Life* magazine."

"Get you," said Ada. "Do you guys want medals, maybe?"

"Ada, that's why they were selected by the CIA," I said. "Right?"

Fresco laughed again, which I took to be a yes. Eva nodded with a smile that was a better answer.

"So what about you two?" I asked. "What are your plans?"

"Once our de-processing is complete, our plans involve getting the hell out, is what," said Fresco. "The studios are all shut down after the fire, of course. There won't be much in production anytime soon." He looked at Eva. "I'm thinking we take a vacation. Somewhere the *Daily News* won't find us."

Eva looked at Fresco and Fresco looked at Eva. He was smiling and so was she, but there was something behind her smile.

"And the CIA?"

"Can go to hell," said Fresco. Then he pursed his lips and winced like he was watching a boxer take a dive under hot lights. "Actually, maybe we should file a report before we go."

"Sounds like a good idea," I said.

"But if you have to include us, feel free to be a little liberal with the facts, if you don't mind," said Ada. "We *are* running a private business, here."

Fresco smiled and nodded and he made his fingers into a little gun shape and he pointed it at one of the computer decks and he clicked his tongue.

I think I liked him. I think I liked them both. They discussed holiday destinations with their backs turned to me while I went to the closet and got out a fresh set of clothes. I cleared my throat when I was done and Eva laughed.

And then she came up to me and gave me a hug, or as best she could, considering her arms didn't go all the way around.

Then Fresco was in on it, too, and I'll be damned if I didn't see a tear in the lug's eye.

After that I led them into the outer office and I showed them the door. Then I opened it and ushered them out and then we said goodbye with them in the hallway and me in the office and when we were done I closed the door.

On my desk was an athletic bag. I opened it. It was full of small gold bars that shone wetly.

"I'm guessing we can keep this," I said.

"You better believe it, Ray," said Ada.

"I don't know about you, Ada, but I need a drink."

"Says the robot," she said. And then she made a sound like she was smoking a cigarette. I laughed and it sounded like someone threading the bit on an industrial drill.

"Actually," I said, "I feel like a root beer float. I know just the place. I won't be long."

As I left the office and locked the door behind me I heard Ada laugh and tell me to knock myself out.

Then I went down to the parking garage and stood there looking at the empty spot where my car was supposed to be.

I smiled on the inside and walked up the exit ramp and onto Hollywood Boulevard.

It looked like a mighty nice day for a walk.

ACKNOWLEDGMENTS

Oh boy, where to start? Hold on to your hats, ladies and gents, because this is a big one.

Made to Kill started with "Brisk Money" and "Brisk Money" started with a little interview I did for *Tor.com* way back when. It was a form interview, the standard shtick for new authors not worth a dime who were lucky enough to get a seat at the big table. There were questions and lots of them and they said I could take my pick. So I did. And the last one on the list was pretty fun. It was: "If you could find one previously undiscovered book by a nonliving author, who would it be? Why?"

Little did I know that my answer to this was going to start me down a road that was long and winding and a heck of a lot of fun. Because I answered the question with the first thing that came into my head: What I really wanted to read and what I really wished did exist was Raymond Chandler's long-lost science fiction epic.

I'm a Chandler fan, big time, and it's always amused me the way Chandler hated science fiction. Hated it. In 1953, he wrote to his agent about it and in the space of 152 words wrote his own little sci-fi vignette that's full of pink pretzels and the rising of the fourth moon and—if you can believe it—what seems to be a computer called

Google. He was proving a point, and the story is meaningless nonsense . . . but it's meaningless nonsense written by Raymond Chandler.

And Raymond Chandler was a genius.

Of course, what Chandler was really doing—well, I'm pretty sure, anyway—was fishing, running this kooky sci-fi thing up the flagpole to see who saluted. Alas, if his agent ever replied, the answer remains unpublished. That's a letter I'd love to see.

But Chandler writing science fiction? Wow. There was a neat idea. And it seems my editor at Tor, Paul Stevens, thought so too, because he said I should write that lost Chandler sci-fi epic. Maybe he was joking and he never told me, but I took him up on his suggestion and the result was a novelette called "Brisk Money," which was published on *Tor.com* in July 2014.

A funny thing happened while I was writing "Brisk Money." I got some more ideas. I'd just met Ray Electromatic, and his boss, Ada, and when I was done with that story I wanted to tell more—a whole novel's worth. No, two novels—screw it, make it *three*.

You're holding the first one, right now.

Paul Stevens was there at the start and really all this is his doing, so he has my thanks from now until eternity. My heartfelt gratitude to everyone else at Tor who took a liking to my little story about a robot who killed people for a living in the Californian sunshine, in particular Irene Gallo for the most amazing art direction in the history of art direction (I mean, come on, just take another look at the cover of this thing. It's okay. I'll wait. You back? The cover is great, right?), Patty Garcia for diabolical master plans and devotion to the Electromatic Detective Agency above and beyond the call of duty, and to my new editor, Miriam Weinberg, who not only loves Ray and Ada as much as I do but also really gets them as much as I do. As an author, I can't ask for any more than that.

Thanks to Will Staehle, who is now firmly established as my artistic wingman (He did the cover, like he does all my covers, but he really went the extra mile on this one. Go take another look. Go!), and to my agent, Stacia J. N. Decker of the Donald Maass Literary Agency, who yet again helped me get this thing up to the next level of literary magic. She also gave this book its perfect, perfect title. Make sure you buy her a drink next time she's in town.

Made to Kill needed research, and lots of it. Not only did that include another close study of the Raymond Chandler canon itself but also of two superb reference works: *The Raymond Chandler Papers: Selected Letters and Nonfiction, 1909–1959,* edited by Tom Hiney and Frank MacShane, and *A Mysterious Something in the Light: The Life of Raymond Chandler,* by Tom Williams.

This book would have been a great deal harder to write if it wasn't for *The Raymond Chandler Map of Los Angeles: A Guide to the Usual & Unusual* from Herb Lester Associates, compiled and described by Kim Cooper with excellent design and illustration from Paul Rogers.

My thanks to the usual (and unusual) suspects: Kim Curran, Joelle Charbonneau, Daryl Gregory, Miranda Jewess, Emma Newman, Alex Segura, Victoria Schwab, Chuck Wendig, and Jen Williams. Thanks to everyone who has supported me both in private and in public. There are too many of you to list and I'm up against a deadline here, so you'll just have to trust me when I say I know who you are and I know what you did and, for some of you anyway, I know where you live. Which means Ray and Ada know where you live, too. Remember that . . .

To my wife, Sandra, whose support and belief and patience are without end. This book is for you.

And finally, to the grand master of detective fiction himself, Raymond Chandler. Thank you. I hope I did okay and I hope *Made to Kill* is, indeed, a scream. This book is for you, too.